September 7, 1870

    Today would have been my father's birthday. Today he would have been thirty-nine. He didn't survive the war. I wonder what it would have been like if he had lived? What would we have been doing tonight?

    Sometimes I think that Abigail, Liam, and Mother don't remember Father well. To them, it has been a lifetime since the war. Abigail and Liam do their mill work, Mother does her housework at the Clatterbucks'. They don't talk about the past.

    But to me, there are times when Father's death seems like only yesterday. I want to reach back to that day, grab my father by his straps in the heat of that dread battle and shout at him. "Stay low! Watch out! Be careful, and come back to us at our farm near Duncannon." Then I come aware again of where I am, and of the years gone. And I set my mind on my work and my duties, so I can help my family up from our poverty. So I can save enough that someday I can quit the mill. I have, as of this day, put away nineteen dollars of which my mother knows nothing. It is hidden behind a loose wallboard in our bedroom. This shall go to pay my college fees someday. It even feels strange to write the word.

    College. It is th

Tor Books by Elizabeth Massie

*Forthcoming

YOUNG FOUNDERS

1870:

NOT WITH OUR BLOOD

Elizabeth Massie

TOR®

A TOM DOHERTY ASSOCIATES BOOK
NEW YORK

This is a work of fiction. All the characters and events portrayed in this book are either products of the author's imagination or are used fictitiously.

YOUNG FOUNDERS #1: 1870: NOT WITH OUR BLOOD

Copyright © 2000 by Elizabeth Massie

A Tor Book
Published by Tom Doherty Associates, LLC
175 Fifth Avenue
New York, NY 10010

www.tor.com

Tor® is a registered trademark of Tom Doherty Associates, LLC.

ISBN: 0-812-59092-9

First edition: March 2000

Printed in the United States of America

0 9 8 7 6 5 4 3 2 1

To Jeni Hurst, a very special person

❧ Introduction ❧

LEELAND IS A fictional mill town, but the cotton textile mills were a very real part of New England in the 1800s, cranking out tons of material to be used across the growing United States. Many of these mills were along the Merrimack River, from Manchester, New Hampshire, to Lowell and Lawrence, Massachusetts. And many of the workers who poured their energies and life's blood into the mills were countless immigrants who had come to America seeking a better life.

During the Civil War the agricultural South had endured much destruction and devastation. Reconstruction was a painful and expensive proposition. But the North, an area already more dependant on industry than farming, had suffered little damage during the war and had little to rebuild. It was a time of rapid growth. Mills and other factories began to flourish. In 1840 manufacturing accounted for less than a fifth of all U.S. production, but by the late

1800s, the United States had become the largest and most competitive industrial nation in the world. Not only did the United States supply goods for its own westward-expanding population, it exported a good deal of its materials across the seas. The need for workers to run the machines in the factories was great.

It was to the United States, the country of opportunity, that many immigrants flocked seeking plentiful jobs, good farmland, and political and religious freedom. They came from Ireland, Germany, Poland, Scandinavia, and Eastern Europe during the mid-1800s. The largest movement of the Irish to the United States occurred between 1840 and 1850, when a famine in their homeland caused a potato crop failure so severe that many had to leave or face starvation and economic ruin. In 1847 alone, 100,000 Irish sailed to the United States to begin anew. And while some founded homesteads in the west, many others believed that by moving to the cities, where the industries were located, they would have a greater chance at gaining the good life.

Today, around five million young Americans between the ages of fourteen and eighteen work at some time during the year. In the 1800s, part-time work would have been considered a luxury that most families couldn't afford. In the 1800s it was not enough for immigrant parents to work while the children went to school or had free time with friends. As more immigrants arrived looking for work, the competition for mill jobs grew fierce. Immigrants were willing to work for less pay in order to secure jobs, which lowered wage levels. For a family to survive, even under the roughest of conditions in the worst slum housing, everyone of age ("of age" meaning anyone older than ten years old) was needed to work. And in spite of the fact that entire families worked hard in hopes of making their lives better, many remained in poverty.

Prejudices against the immigrants grew as the industries grew. Some Americans, even those whose parents had been immigrants, blamed the new arrivals for problems such as poor wages, crime, overcrowding, and even immoral influences. The American Party, sometimes called the Know-Nothing Party, wanted to halt immigration and make it difficult for immigrants to become citizens.

Not everyone saw the immigrants as evil, however. Labor unions and "radical" journalists hoped to end long hours, terrible working conditions, and child labor in the factories by making society and lawmakers aware of these issues. In 1860, Pemberton Mills in Lawrence, Massachusetts, collapsed. The weight of the machines proved to be too much for the structure and many workers were killed or seriously maimed by the falling machinery. This disaster brought media attention to poorly constructed, poorly planned buildings. Newspapers published shocking, graphically vivid articles. But it took a long time before factories started improving conditions and longer still before the changes were consistent throughout New England and the rest of the country.

And so, in 1870, people still lived in crowded, rundown tenement apartments. They rose before dawn and walked to the mills where they were locked in rooms filled with dust, lint, and the relentless pounding of machinery. The mills were places where materials were produced and tragic accidents occurred. There was a short break in the day so that workers could eat in the aisles between the machines. They returned home after the day after twelve or fourteen hours of work. They went to sleep, only to rise as the mill bell clanged to begin the routine once more.

1

July 6, 1863

Something is wrong. Mother hasn't come back from the barn. Abigail and Liam pestered me all afternoon to go out and see her, but Mother told me that we all must stay in the house. And so we have.

It's been nine hours. What is she doing out there?

I think Abigail and Liam are asleep now. I can't hear them talking anymore. They were both crying and crying and it made my head hurt so bad that I gave them some leftover stew for supper and sent them off to their mattresses in the loft. Liam went right away, but Abigail argued with me. She said she was nine and not a baby, so she didn't have to do as I said. I told her Father is dead now, so she has to listen to me, because I was the man of the house now, even if I was a year younger than she. I threw a biscuit at her and it hit her on the head and she stamped her foot, screamed at me, then climbed the ladder to the loft.

I cleaned up the bowls, but I couldn't eat any stew myself. My stomach hurts bad.

It's dark and Mother is still in the barn. From the table where I sit I can see out across the dark yard. Her lantern is burning in there.

This morning we got word that Father was killed in a battle at Gettysburg. They are bringing the body home for burial in a few days.

Gettysburg. It seems so far away. Father has been away nearly a year now. Mother hated to see him go. 'It's not your fight,' she had said.

Father told her he could not abide a system in which one man was made the master of another. He said, being Irish, he'd had enough of that with the English.

'This war is every man's fight,' he said.

I wanted to join the Union Army with Father. But he said 'no.' I was too young. And he needed me to help with the farm. He rustled my hair and smiled. 'There will be plenty of chores to do when I get back.'

Now, he's never coming back.

Mother thanked the man who brought the message, then turned to the three of us and told us to stay in the house. She didn't cry. She told us we best not cry, either. Then she put on her shawl, took a lantern, and went to the barn. Nugget tried to go in the barn with her, but she pushed him out with her foot.

Widow Muncy is dead. It happened last year when her husband was killed in the war. They found her all puffed up and purple in the rafters of her cabin. I wonder if she has hanged herself from grief.

Father is dead, too. If I think of it, I can't bear it. And now Mother may be dead as well. So many have died already. When will it end?

The politicians promised it would be a short fight. That was two years ago. And it doesn't appear that the rebel soldiers are ready to quit.

It hasn't gone well for the Union. People are growing tired of the fight. But I support President Lincoln. Slavery is an abomination. No man has the right to make a slave of another. Father said that.

And I believe him. What are we going to do now? I am the oldest. I am supposed to know, but I don't. We do not own this farm. We lease it with money we make from raising our chickens and cows. I can't raise them by myself. We will lose our home! What am I supposed to do?

❧ 2 ❧

PATRICK THOMAS O'NEILL put his paper and pen away inside the cupboard, gave one more glance out the window at the barn, then climbed the ladder to join his sister and brother for sleep. In the darkness he felt his way along the rough wooden floor to his own mattress. He kicked off his shoes, leaned over, and opened the loft window to let in a cool Pennsylvania breeze. Then he lay down and drew his legs up beneath his quilt.

But sleep didn't come for many hours.

July 12, 1863
We buried Father today. A wagon arrived at the farm this morning, with a private and a lieutenant named Marshall. Mother came outside when the wagon pulled into the yard. Lt. Marshall nodded and lifted off his hat. Mother looked over his shoulder to the wagon. When Mother saw the pine box I heard her inhale deeply, but she said not a word.

"What is it?" asked Liam. "It's Father," I said. "Now hush."

Mother called to me then. "Patrick, bring your Father off that wagon and up that hill just below the oak."

Abigail began to cry softly. Mother turned and glared at her coldly.

Lt. Marshall stepped aside. The private tumbled down from the wagon and helped me slide the coffin out the back. It was not heavy. "This way," I said. Our eyes met, and I realized he was not that much older than me.

We carried the box across the small meadow and lay it down under the shade of a sprawling oak. A hole had been dug. I guess Mother had attended to it. We stood around the box in a silent circle as the lieutenant read a few prayers from an old leather Bible. It did not seem possible that Father was actually inside the box. Dead. That I would never see him again.

It was like a strange dream I was in.

The lieutenant closed his book, and he and the private remounted their wagon and drove away. After an awkward silence, I steered Abigail and Liam back to the house. In the doorway, I turned to look back at Mother.

She lingered at the grave a long time, like a stone statue in the shade of the great oak, its limbs spread over her as if in comfort. Then her shoulders began to shake, and she dropped slowly to her knees.

I stepped inside the house, and closed the door.

When Patrick awoke, there was a puddle of morning sunlight on the loft floor. Patrick rubbed his eyes and sat up. Abigail and five-year-old Liam were still sleeping. Patrick wasn't surprised. Yesterday had been hell. *Today,* he thought, *might be even worse.*

Patrick stretched his shoulders and clutched his quilt around himself. The quilt was a special one, made for him by his mother the year he was born, embroidered with his name and his birthday and all sorts of animals and flowers. Usually the quilt offered comfort. But not today. And even though it was stuffy in the loft, Patrick was cold.

Mother must still be in the barn, he thought, shivering as much from fear of what had happened as with the cold. *It's been almost a week now. What can she do doing?*

Quietly he slipped into his clothes and went down the ladder. He stoked the coals in the hearth from yesterday's fire but only got a few red sparks. He would have to go outside for wood if he was going to fix a breakfast or heat water for washing linens.

But Mother had said to stay in the house.

He opened the door.

Nugget raced in, wagging his tail and dancing on his paws as if happy to be remembered. Patrick gave the brown mutt a quick pat on the head, then looked out the door, across the wide garden to the barn.

I have to find out what's going on, he told himself. *I have to see what Mother's done.*

He went out onto the covered porch, closing the door behind him. The air was warm. Soon it would be stiflingly hot. The broad leaves of the cornstalks in the garden stood motionless; the pole beans were ripe and heavy on the tangle of woven sticks. Patrick straightened his suspenders, set his jaw, and marched across the lumpy ground of the garden to the barn. If she was dead, he couldn't think what he would do.

Creeping to the open door, he took a breath. He looked at his feet. He looked at the sky. And then he looked into the barn.

Lucy O'Neill was there, alive and bustling. Her sleeves were rolled up and her apron was twisted slightly askew. There was a hammer in her hand. Dust swirled in golden sparkles of the filtered sunshine. There were nails clamped in Lucy's lips and a scowl of determination on her face.

She was repairing the old wagon. Patrick watched for a few minutes, then went back to the house.

Abigail and Liam were up, still in nightclothes, watching from the porch. Abigail hadn't brushed her hair. Liam's hair stuck up like the brush of a rooster.

"She's fixing the wagon," Patrick said.

"What for?" asked Abigail.

"I don't know."

"We going somewhere?" asked Liam.

"I don't know," said Patrick. "Let's have some oatmeal."

By noon, as Abigail was hanging out clothes to dry and Liam and Patrick were in the garden weeding, Mother came out of the barn. She strolled straight to the porch, called her three children to her, and explained that they would leave the farm and go to New Jersey.

"My brother Robert lives there," she said, weariness tugging on the sides of her mouth. "You don't remember my brother, but that is no matter. He will help us. That is what family is for. I will write him and let him know that we will work for our board. They needn't worry that we'll be a burden. They have cows and goats. You children know about animal care. You'll do as you are told, be the command from me or anyone in that household."

"New Jersey?" Abigail asked, pressing her hand to the bodice of her dress as if she was going to be ill.

"Yes," said Mother. "There will be no mourning for what we have lost here, because longing does no good. We must go on."

Liam began to cry, and Mother let him. But when Abigail's eyes teared up and Patrick put his fist to his mouth, she snapped, "I do not need this of you! I need your help and your strength. Change doesn't have to be a bad thing. Now, Patrick! I want you to write a flyer this very afternoon, telling of our need to sell. Then take it to the mercantile and tack it on the wall for all to see."

Patrick did as he had been told. He also secretly sold his father's good boots to the man at the next farm and kept the money hidden in the well-worn leather haversack his father had carried with him during the war.

Two months later, the O'Neill family left the farm with the wagon and horse and dog, two chairs, mattress ticks, and a chest, heading for Robert Norman's New Jersey farm.

3

December 21, 1864

I'm sick of this place. It hasn't gotten better, only worse. Nugget ran away. Nobody likes us. We O'Neills are just a bother to the Normans. I have to tell my stories and jokes to Abigail and Liam when no one else is around because they think a child should be seen and not heard. Back in Pennsylvania, before Father went to war, he taught me to read and write. Although there are many men who have never had the chance to learn their letters, my father believed it was one thing a man needed to know in order to do better in life. My favorite books were Robinson Crusoe *and* Gulliver's Travels, *two tales of adventure! But here they have only a few books, and would be angry if they knew I borrowed them to read at night. They know nothing of adventure.*

I think grouchy old adults shouldn't have to be seen or heard.

The work here on the Normans' farm is not hard,

only dull. The animals here in New Jersey are just like the ones we had back in Pennsylvania. But even though I've tried for some time now, I still hate Uncle Robert and Aunt Sadie. I hate them! Mother says we have to obey, and we do. We only have one cramped bedroom for all of us, and we have to smile and say thank you for every crumb. Uncle Robert never speaks to children except to yell, and Aunt Sadie is afraid of her own shadow. She spooks Liam and Abigail at night, telling them tales of ghosts in the attic and in the well.

The story that scares them the most is one she tells about the old woman who used to live at a farm nearby. The old woman had white hair and white eyes. The old woman would wait until she could see children from her upstairs window, then would beckon them with her bony fingers to come over for cakes. When the children got close enough, she would reach down her arms, which could stretch ten feet, and grab the children. She would then cook them for dinner.

A few nights ago, I went outside when everyone was asleep and held a mop covered with a white cloth up to Aunt Sadie's bedroom window and tapped on the glass lightly. She awoke, saw the mop in the moonlight, and screamed that the demons were after her. I hid in the shed while everyone searched the yard for the demon. I laughed, but couldn't share the trick with anyone else or I'd be in serious trouble. When Liam is older, I'll tell him.

It would be more fun if Uncle Robert and Aunt Sadie had children to play with, but Mother says God hasn't blessed them.

Good news. The War may soon be over. General

Grant is chasing Lee back through Virginia. It's only a matter of time now. Then it will be over.

I wonder what will happen then? Uncle Robert grumbles about falling prices for farm goods, now that the war is coming to an end. I heard him talking with a neighbor about something called a "depression." I'm not sure I know what that means. When I asked Uncle Robert, he barked, "It means hard times are coming!"

The Negroes are free. Thank God. It makes me think Father's death was not in vain. He would be so proud. What would he think of me then? Sometimes I wonder if freedom means so much when you are poor. Like us. This journal paper is poor quality, but it is all I can get. Father used to buy me paper when he would go to town, but, of course, he is gone. I used the money I got from selling his boots to get these sheets and this ink. I feel bad about it because I never told Mother I had the money, but I had to be able to get paper. I have to be able to write.

I am going to be a real writer someday. I'll make up stories of adventure and excitement! One day I'll be paid for my stories and my poems. I'll be famous, and will help my family buy a new farm. My father will know it, even though he is dead. And Liam will be so proud of me. I'm twelve now. How old does one need to be before he can be a real writer?

I wonder.

It will be Christmas soon. I think it might be a dreary holiday this year. Father used to make Christmas a jolly time.

I pray there are beautiful candles and wonderful food in heaven at Christmastime.

4

By LATE 1867, talk of the war was beginning to fade. Patrick had read in newspapers that the South was having a hard time rebuilding homes and lives due to the great destruction and lack of industry. But in New Jersey, people worked and farmed and went to church as usual. Aunt Sadie, who had said she would never be able to have children, bore twins, two little girls with red hair and squinty baby eyes. Sadie swore to anyone close enough to listen that the pain of the birth had nearly killed her.

It was then that Uncle Robert made it clear that the strain of too many people on too little land was making Sadie's tribulation even greater. By the end of the harvest in August, the O'Neills packed up and prepared to leave in search of yet another, stranger life.

"We need housing and jobs," Mother said. She was sitting with her children in their narrow bedroom at the back of the Normans' house the night before

they left. All four were on Mother's bed, the bedside lantern battling feebly with the night gloom, a
moth battling feebly with the lantern. Mother had a
newspaper, and was pointing at an announcement.
"There are many textile mills in Massachusetts which
are in need of workers. You children are strong and
healthy. We'll do well."

"What's a textile mill?" asked Liam.

"Makes cloth," said Mother.

"How?"

"I don't know," she said. "Doesn't matter. They'll
show you. Article here says that many mills up north
let go thousands of workers during the war, thinking
they couldn't run their mills to profit. Now that the
war's done, they're running full again, selling not
only to our own country but other countries. There
is much money to make in the mills, and they need
workers. They're filling up with immigrants, but
there may well be room for a Pennsylvania family."

"If we have to move, I want to move south," said
Abigail. "Father had a cousin in Virginia. Can't we
go there? I don't want to work in a mill."

"The South is poor," said Mother. "One reason
they lost the war is because they didn't have factories
to make what they needed in bulk for their soldiers.
Clothes. Weapons. And now the little they did have
has been burned or knocked down. The southern
plantations are producing cotton, but the money's
not there, it is in the cloth the cotton produces. And
the cloth is made in the factories. We'd be worse off
than we are now if we went south. Our only hope is
in the North."

"I don't like the sound of it all," said Abigail.

Mother said, "We're going to find us a mill."

"What mill, Mother?" asked Liam, leaning into Patrick, and Patrick putting his arm about his little brother's shoulder. "Where is the mill?"

Lucy didn't answer. It was clear she was thinking this over. Patrick said to his sister and brother, "This will be good. We can go and make some real money. We'll start over, and soon we'll be able to get a new farm, all our own."

"Really?" asked Liam.

"Of course really," said Patrick.

"We'll go to Leeland," said Lucy at last, as if she hadn't heard Patrick. Then she turned down the lantern, shooed the children off the bed, and said no more.

The next morning, after a hurried breakfast and good-byes, the O'Neills steered their horse and wagon onto the rain-rutted dirt path, heading northward.

Leeland, Massachusetts, which was on the Merrimack River just southwest of Lawrence, was different from other towns Patrick had seen. It was not a farming town. It was an industrial town. When they first rounded the bend in the road and looked down the gentle slope of the hill, Mother pulled the horse up short and all four of the family stared, eyes wide. Abigail, sitting in front with her mother, caught her breath audibly. In the back, Liam and Patrick got up on their knees.

The first thing that struck Patrick was the smokestacks. They were dark and tall, pointing to the sky. They were part of the enormous factory compound along the river. Within the walled compound were several single-story brick buildings, a tall bell tower, and one main brick building, which was four stories high and quite long. Windows dotted the tall building's sides. Even from the top of the knoll where the O'Neills sat, the huge building seemed to groan with its mysterious inner workings. Two canals and a train track ran through gateways into the compound.

Patrick held his breath and clutched his journal to his chest. He had been writing in the wagon whenever there had been a stretch of straight road, but much of what he'd written was a jumbled, scratched mess.

"I don't like it," said Liam to his mother.

Patrick tried to picture his family working here, making lots of money and becoming rich. It was hard to imagine. The place was so stark.

"Train brings in cotton and takes away the cloth when it's done," said Mother matter-of-factly to her children in the wagon.

"I see," Liam said. He snuggled against Patrick as if he didn't really want to see at all.

Outside the wall of the compound and up the hillside were several rows of smaller, single-story wooden buildings. Squinting in the sunlight, Patrick could see clothes on lines behind these buildings.

He wrote quickly in the journal.

Do the workers live here in these little houses? They aren't very welcoming, but at least they are close to the mill. Maybe workers can live there for free. That would be good. We could save our money up faster, my family can buy a new farm, and I can go to college and become a writer! We won't have to stay here long!

Across the river from the mill compound was the town of Leeland. The sky that hung over it was not crisp and bright like the sky over the farmland. It was blue, but a tainted blue.

A dirty blue.

Lucy clucked to the horse to get him going again. Patrick glanced at Abigail. Abigail glanced back at Patrick. The road was rutted, and reluctantly Patrick put his journal aside.

The wagon descended the knoll, moving by the mill compound and across a community bridge. The Merrimack River below the bridge was brown and rippling. Parallel to the community bridge, about one hundred feet down the river, was a covered bridge that led from the town across to the mill compound. A workers' bridge, Patrick imagined. No one was on that bridge now. Patrick tried to picture himself strolling that bridge, but couldn't. Even his good imagination was struggling here, trying to place himself and his family in this town. In that mill.

At an open-air market in town, women argued and men shouted and children laughed and cried, their voices all becoming a blurred, discordant melody. Vegetables sat in baskets and buckets; salted meats hung on hooks. Clearly this produce was far from fresh. Patrick stared as the wagon rattled by. He watched the faces of those in the market, hoping to see someone turn and smile at him, bidding him welcome. But they were all too busy with their own chores.

"That's all right," he said to himself. "We'll get along just fine."

"What did you say?" asked Liam.

"I asked if you saw those apples. Aren't they fine now?" said Patrick. Liam nodded.

They stopped on a side street, and Lucy told the children to stay put. She climbed out and spoke to a woman who was pouring a bucket of soapy water into the street. The woman pointed to a tall, wooden building on the other side of the road. Lucy knocked on the door and a man came out. Patrick strained to listen to what the man was saying to his mother.

"Twenty years ago you'd get your boarding in a decent house. The company would provide it. But the cotton mill has expanded so much they can't do that no more. You got to live wherever you can find space. If you can find it at all."

Lucy stood straight and adjusted her shawl. "Those homes behind the mill?"

"Those are the old boardinghouses," said the man, pulling at one end of his greasy mustache. "But they're filled. No chance there. Now workers rent from private tenement owners here in the town proper. Like me. Used to be it was mostly farm girls in the mills, back in the forties. Girls who needed money to send their families, and some who just wanted to be a bit more independent than their farming sisters. These girls would live in them boardinghouses and have meals cooked for them. Disciplined, they were, going to church regularly, and in at proper hours. Mills knew what to do to keep them in line. You won't find that now, though. The company ain't got time to worry 'bout girls out after ten at night. Ain't got the desire to pay matrons to watch over the girls and cook meals. Those were good days, yes, sir."

Lucy said, "We don't care about twenty years ago."

"Of course," said the man suddenly, his face twitching as though he was trying not to laugh. "There's the shanties outside town, up west end. There's Irish out there, and the French-Canadians, too. You want I should find you some boards for making a shanty shack?"

Lucy pressed, "Is there work here now, and are there lodgings?"

"Work, most likely, but boarding, I don't know. I'll have to check."

"Thank you," said Lucy.

Lucy came back over the road and climbed into the wagon. The man walked ahead, on foot.

"Who is that?" asked Liam.

"Landlord," said Lucy. Slapping the reins on the horse's flanks, Lucy went silent again.

The wagon went down a street with a marker reading "Charlotte Road" and then down an alley and around the back of a four-story wooden building full of open windows and noisy tenants. Clothing and bed linens hung from the windows and were draped on the railings of the stair landings. A child leaned out of a fourth-floor window and emptied a bucket of excrement.

The landlord skipped out of the way as the human waste hit the alley with a wet splat. Patrick gawked. "Got to watch out for that," the landlord said.

The flat offered to the O'Neills was on the third floor. Lucy hobbled the horse, and the family ascended two flights of rickety exterior steps, then through an open doorway into a dim, musty hall.

The landlord unlocked the door and everyone stared inside. Liam was the only one to pinch his nose and say, "Stinks!"

"It certainly does," Patrick whispered to his brother. Patrick was used to the scents of a farm, of cow manure and mud and straw and sunshine. But this smelled of the people who had lived here before them. It smelled of sickness and decay.

The flat consisted of only two rooms, a kitchen with a window overlooking the alleyway below, and a bedroom with no window at all. There was a cast-iron cookstove provided, which seemed to satisfy Lucy. Wood, the landlord said, could be purchased at the market or from a cart that came around every morning on Charlotte Road. The flat's walls were thin, and Patrick could hear an argument next door. Riding the sunlight that filtered through the kitchen window was thick, airborne mill grit.

"You have the Keiths across from you, and the Pattersons next to you," said the landlord. "You'll meet them shortly, I suppose."

Lucy nodded. "Neighbors," she said.

Patrick studied the warped wood of the floor of the kitchen and whispered to Abigail, "We'll make it here. We'll be all right." Abigail looked at him and shook her head.

The landlord accepted the wagon and horse as payment for three months' rent.

"We'll make do," Lucy had said as the wagon and horse were led away and the O'Neills watched from the landing on the steps. "We have our arms and legs to work."

That night, when everyone seemed to have settled down to sleep, Patrick went outside and sat on the wooden steps with his pad and pen.

October 3, 1867

Neighbors? The landlord says we have neighbors, but I'd argue with him if I could! Neighbors live in houses down roads, not in stinky boxes next to each other! How can we call this home? How can anyone? I'd hoped this would be better than living with Uncle Robert and Aunt Sadie, but now I don't know.

We are here, in Leeland. I don't like it.

It's very strange here.

I can see the stars overhead. They are blurry and pale, but they are there, nonetheless.

I'm fourteen, almost a man. My mother needs me. So does Abigail, and especially Liam. I know I will do what I have to so we can get by. And I'll keep on writing. I'll never give that up. Father wouldn't have wanted me to give it up. He always knew I wanted to be a writer, even when I was just a little boy.

Some things will never change. Like the stars. Like me.

Tomorrow I will look for work at the mill.

THE LEELAND MILLS
1870

❧ 5 ❧

WHEN THE GREAT machines in the mill shuddered to a halt for the noon dinner break, Patrick heard the child's scream. His fingers drew up from the cloth he was folding into wooden crates for shipment. His neck tightened; his heart pounded. Around his face, dust flew like insects.

The cry had come from beyond the storage room door where Patrick and the other cloth packers worked, out where the early September sun cast spots of light through the overcast sky, where the train tracks lay along the mill yard, awaiting the cars that would carry away the crates of cotton cloth.

"Hear that?" Patrick asked Mr. Steele, the old man who packed crates next to him.

"What?"

"The child."

"No."

It might be Liam, Patrick thought. *It can't be Liam, not again!*

Patrick moved quickly to the open door. He squeezed through the towering stacks of crates with their Leeland Mills trademark emblem stenciled on the lids and the mountainous bolts of fabric that had been brought in on hardcarts from the finishing rooms. He swiped at his eyes as he went, trying to dislodge the grime that made clear sight difficult.

Of course it's not Liam injured. So many children work here. It could be any one of them.

"Where you going there, boy!" This was Mr. Depper, the second hand. He had been scolding another packer for some infraction Patrick could only guess was slow work, but when the second hand saw Patrick pass, he stopped short and frowned.

"I need some air."

"Air?" called Mr. Depper. His voice was as irritating as a mosquito's buzz. "You got plenty air in here! You ain't up in one of them spinning or weaving rooms where the windows are nailed shut, are you? What you got to complain about?"

Patrick didn't turn around, but he didn't talk back either. It would do no good to get in trouble for insubordination.

"Don't you go outside, boy. You know the train ain't here yet!"

Patrick stopped at the door and looked out at the mill yard. It was hard to see at first. Squinting, he put his hand up to shield his eyes. Then he saw them. Standing beside the tracks was a man and a crying boy. Every few seconds the man would shake the boy and the boy would scream. He was small, about Liam's size. He wore short, ragged pants, a dirty white shirt, suspenders, and cracked leather shoes. The boy held his right hand in his left. Most likely he had been wounded by one of the machines.

"Patrick O'Neill!" shouted Mr. Depper.

"Just a moment!" Patrick shouted back.

There was a piece of cloth around the boy's hand, bound tightly. The unbleached cloth was now scarlet. The boy was hurt badly. Somehow his hand had been smashed.

Patrick's stomach twisted. He remembered Liam losing his left forefinger the year before. He'd been cleaning the floors in Carding Room #1, collecting lint with a broom. When he'd lost his balance, he had stumbled, catching his finger in the gears of a sharp-toothed machine. The finger had been amputated at the second knuckle.

Patrick did not know this wounded boy, not that there was any reason he would. Liam talked about different children he knew at the mill, some of whom worked as doffers in Spinning Room #4 on the third floor, but Patrick had never put names to faces because he never really saw the worker children's faces. He only saw them in a blur, running messages or carting fluff and dust down from the weaving and spinning rooms, and in particular, wheeling the handcarts in from the finishing room so the men could crate the material for shipment on the next train.

Outside, the man shook the boy one more time, then stalked away, his boots sending up dusty divots. The boy hung his head and walked off in the direction of the mill's offices.

If he's too badly hurt, Patrick thought, *he'll be dismissed. It will be his own bad luck.*

Shaking his head, Patrick walked back to his work station. He could hear another packer say quietly as he passed, "A shame, truly, that child out there. Another crime ignored by this man-eating business."

Mr. Steele was seated on a crate, eating a roll. "Let it go, boy," he said. "It's not for you to worry about the problems of another."

Patrick looked at the old man. Mr. Steele was tall, pale, and bald. The only hairs he had grew like wild gray weeds on his chin and upper lip. His arms were knotted and sweat-slicked.

"Maybe," Patrick said. He picked up the leather haversack in which he carried his lunch and took out an apple. He took a bite, carried his cup to the bucket by the wall and filled it with water, then went back and sat on the crate next to Mr. Steele.

"How old are you now, boy?"

"Sixteen," said Patrick. He swallowed the apple bite and washed it down with the coppery-tasting water.

"You been here how long?"

"'Bout four years."

"Thought so," said Mr. Steele. "And you're old enough to know that you have your own matters to tend to. We can't save the world. A man's got to work and earn his keep, and you can't do much more than that."

Patrick didn't answer. He didn't care to have conversations with Mr. Steele, because the man was always trying to tell him what to do. He acted as though he thought he was Patrick's father even though he was not married and had no children. Mr. Steele claimed to have been an overseer in a mill up in Lawrence when he was a younger man, but Patrick didn't believe him. Why would an overseer be reduced to the tedious job of packer here in Leeland? It made no sense, and Mr. Steele was not inclined to explain.

I wish it was Wednesday, Patrick thought. On Wednesdays, with the permission of Mr. Spilman, the packing room overseer, Patrick was allowed to hurry up the outer staircase to the third floor to dine with Abigail and Liam, both of whom worked in Spinning Room #4. This was a rare and for the most part unheard-of practice. Most workers were confined to their space for the many relentless hours of work, forbidden to even take a breath of fresh air through a door or window. But each week Patrick secretly gave Mr. Spilman a few pennies from his pay, and Liam was liked well enough by his own Mr. Gilbert to allow the practice to go on. But today was Friday and so he would eat alone, as long as Mr. Steele kept his thoughts to himself and stayed on his own crate.

Dinner today was the usual, cheese and a hard roll. Water was taken from the buckets in the corner of the room, drawn and brought in by storage-room errand boys.

As he finished the apple and pulled out a piece of hard cheese, Patrick wondered about the family of the injured boy.

"He will go home and mend," Patrick whispered to the cheese in his hand. "If he's lucky, he can return as Liam did, to clean or sweep or doff the bobbins. If he can keep up the pace and not be slowed by the injury, he shouldn't lose pay for it."

Suddenly the machines on the mill thundered back into gear. Patrick stood, brushed cheese crumbs from his legs, stretched his neck to pull out a cramp, and lifted a bolt of cloth to fold.

6

I̵T WAS NEARING eight-thirty when Patrick, Abigail, and Liam crossed the covered mill workers'
bridge over the Merrimack River and plodded up
rocky Burris Street on their way home. Most of the
shops on the street were closed. The only store open
was the company store, Leeland Supplies, just off the
bridge by the river. A few operatives came out with
their purchases, but none of the O'Neills had either
the money or the energy to shop. There were very
few other pedestrians.

Although it was already September, fall was hard
to detect in the middle of town. Not a cool breeze
found the street tonight, not a hint of the cinnamon
smell of autumn. The few scraggly maple trees at
roadside had not a single red or orange leaf to share
with passersby.

The three O'Neills walked close together. It was a
good idea, since an occasional children's gang might
decide to attack and rob lone people out after dark.

Abigail, a willowy girl of eighteen with light brown hair, braided and pinned, held her broadcloth skirt and apron up to keep them from dragging in the puddles on the road. Liam, nearly thirteen, with Patrick's dark brown hair and bright blue eyes, wearily threw pebbles into the puddles to watch them splash.

Gaslights hissed on the street corners, throwing shadows back into alleyways.

The tenement in which the O'Neills lived was a good mile from the river, up the long stretch of Burris Street, then south down narrow Charlotte Road. On both sides of Charlotte Road were three- and four-story tenements. The shadows were black as tar, as no streetlights had been erected here. Except for occasional spots from oil lamps and candles in unshaded windows, Patrick, Abigail, and Liam walked in the darkness. They stepped carefully to keep from twisting ankles or stepping in horse manure.

"You haven't said a word since we left the mill, Patrick," said Liam. "What's wrong?" He punched his brother lightly on the arm.

"Oh, nothing," said Patrick.

"It's something," Liam said. "Usually you tell us jokes or stories. Something."

"I don't have any jokes tonight," said Patrick.

"Why not?"

Patrick sighed. He loved his little brother's admiration and his sister's respect. But tonight he kept thinking of the injured boy. He kept thinking about Mr. Steele's comments. It made him feel tired and discouraged. He hated that feeling.

"Then tell us a story you've told before. Tell the

one you made up about the overseer who falls in the river and is caught by the giant crayfish," said Liam.

Patrick shook his head.

"Then the one about the farmer who invents a spinning machine to spin honeysuckle vines into cloth, but then can't get the machine to stop and his house and farm are swallowed up."

"No," said Patrick.

"But why not?"

"A boy was hurt today," said Patrick. "Did you hear about it?"

"No," said Liam.

"Did you, Abigail?"

Abigail said, "I think so. But I don't know who it was. Some careless child, I suppose. I heard it happened right before the noon dinner break in one of the weaving rooms upstairs. The boy should have been watching out for himself, but clearly he didn't. Why should he have sympathy? I heard no word about him after that. I suppose he must have been all right."

"I don't think he was all right," Patrick mumbled. "And I don't want to talk about it."

"Do you wonder what it would be like to travel on that railroad across the whole country?" asked Liam, his voice rising with the new topic of conversation. He paced his steps with Patrick, taking big strides like his older brother. Abigail had fallen a few yards behind, watching her steps. "Polly told me today that she is going to go to California with her parents as soon as they have the money. There is gold there, and so much land. Isn't she lucky?"

"I suppose she is," said Patrick. Polly Bruce was a

fourteen-year-old girl who worked in Spinning Room #4 with Abigail and Liam. She was a gangly thing with a terrible cough. Her father was one of the drunkards who littered the streets at night. Her mother had a severe case of consumption, which flooded her lungs with mucus and made breathing difficult. Patrick had once heard Polly tell another operative that her father had saved General Ulysses Grant's life in the battle of Shiloh. Of course, just a day earlier, Polly had told Patrick that her father had never set foot outside of Massachusetts because he didn't dare be too far away from his father-in-law, who had thousands of dollars and would not give him a cent if he ever left the bedside of Polly's mother.

Patrick shook his head. Liam was smart but young and easily swayed by exciting stories.

"All right," Patrick said at last. "I'll give you a story. A new one." Anything at this point was better than having to listen to wild tales of Polly Bruce. Patrick began making up a story as he walked. "There once was a flea. He lived on a shaggy little mutt. But one day the owner of the mutt decided it would be so much fancier if he were shaved muzzle to tail tip. Of course, this left the flea without a home."

Liam skipped a step and hooked his thumbs under his suspender straps. "Good! Keep on!"

"The flea was out of his place now, and didn't know what to do. Certainly there were other dogs, but they weren't home. And so the flea decided he would somehow need to go about gluing hair back onto his now bald flat."

Suddenly Abigail grabbed Patrick's shoulder. "The

witch woman is watching us again!" she whispered.

Patrick's head snapped left. There, in a second-floor tenement window, with pale light outlining her, were the head and shoulders of an old woman. The tangled hairs on her head stood out against the light like old cobwebs. One gnarled hand was held up to the window, fingers scrabbling and twitching as if they were cursing the O'Neills. The shadows of the hand on the street at Patrick's feet looked like an enormous, deadly spider.

"Don't look at her!" hissed Liam.

Patrick stopped dead in the street. He stared at the old woman in the window. This was the fourth night in a row she had been waiting, it seemed, for the O'Neills to come home from the mill; the fourth night she had watched them, glaring at them.

"It's like Aunt Sadie's witch!" said Liam. "She wants to suck out our souls!"

"Patrick, run!" said Abigail. She came around Patrick and shook him by the arm. "Now!"

"She'll put a spell on us! She'll let down her hair and catch us!" said Liam.

The woman tilted her head and her wild, white hair rippled. Gooseflesh raced up the backs of Patrick's arms and neck. His heart kicked into a fast, painful rhythm. But still, he could not look away.

"Patrick!" snapped Abigail.

The old woman's other hand came up and linked fingers with the first, making a single bony, wrinkled knot. Her mouth opened slowly.

"She's cursing us!" screeched Liam. "Put your hands over your ears!"

All three did so, and they raced the rest of the distance up Charlotte Road, away from the demon-woman to their own brick tenement and their own tiny third-floor flat.

❧ 7 ❧

September 7, 1870

Lucky. Mr. Steele said the boy who was hurt today
would be lucky if he could return to work like Liam
did after his accident. Lucky used to have a different
meaning. Before coming to Leeland, lucky meant finding a lost coin in the cabin floor or the river not rising
all the way to the barn after a long, hard rain. Lucky
was how I felt when I watched the birth of a healthy
new foal or finding that Mother had made an apple
pie for supper.

Now lucky means staying alive.

I keep thinking of the boy who was hurt today. Did
he have a mother who will cry? A father who will curse
the mill and the men who owned it? Will a sister want
to strike on the boy's behalf, or a brother write a letter
to a newspaper about the horrors of the factories?

No, probably not. Well, the mother will cry, but the
sister won't strike and the brother won't write an article. The sister needs her work; the brother is illiterate.

The father may curse in private, but he knows his family should stay where they are and not raise a ruckus. Survival is at stake.

Today would have been my father's birthday. Today he would have been thirty-nine. He didn't survive the war. I wonder what it would have been like if he had lived. What would we have been doing tonight?

I am different from my father in some ways. I can't picture myself a soldier as I know I don't have the temperament for battle as he did. But I often fancy I favor him in looks. It would have been no disgrace. His hair was as dark as the riverbank mud, his eyes blue as a clear stream. I would wear whiskers such as his if Mother would allow, but she still sees me as too young, in spite of my upcoming seventeenth birthday this December. Many boys younger than I sport manly beards. The last time I tried to grow whiskers I got by four days, then Mother said I looked like a pincushion and off they came. I think she's forgotten that Father had his beard when he was seventeen and they fell in love.

Sometimes I think that Abigail, Liam, and Mother don't remember Father well. To them it has been a lifetime since the war. Abigail and Liam do their mill work, Mother does her housework at the Clatterbucks'. They don't talk about the past.

But to me, there are times when Father's death seems like only yesterday. I want to reach back to that day, grab my father by his straps in the heat of that dread battle, and shout at him, "Stay low! Watch out! Be careful, and come back to us at our farm near Duncannon." Then I become aware again of where I am, and of the years gone. And I set my mind on my work and my duties, so I can help my family up from our poverty. So I can save enough that someday I can quit the mill. I have, as of this day, put away $19, of which my mother knows nothing. It is hidden behind a loose wall board in our bedroom. This shall go to pay my college fees someday.

College. It is there I'll become a writer.

But some nights, sorrow hangs on my back like an old jacket too tight to shed, like pine sap in my hair, too thick and old to wash away, like the stings of hornets, red and hot, swelling up more each time I scratch at them. Tonight college seems like a ridiculous fantasy, as slippery as a catfish.

The Leeland moon is watching me now. It is a cold, unblinking eye, so unlike the kind moon of the country. I think it can read my journal over my shoulder.

I hope someday to become a writer and make his spirit proud.

Father, I miss you.

8

PATRICK PUT HIS journal aside and pushed it back against the crumbling brick wall of his tenement so the random winds wouldn't catch the pages and spin them like dead leaves to the alley. Paper was a treasure, and he couldn't afford to lose a single sheet. He had to tell his mother he made fewer cents than he really did at the mill so he could squirrel away a precious yet small amount to save for college and also buy paper for his journal. There were a lot of things he had learned since his father had died. One thing was the importance of his family, because he could not imagine making it through this mill life alone. Another was how to lie about little things.

Patrick sat with his legs dangling off the landing on the back stairs, his arms laced through the balusters, staring at the garbage-littered alley two floors below. The alley was dark but not silent. There were the growling sounds of stray cats, seeking out scraps of food among trash and discarded boards, and the argument of drunk men in the building next door. Every so often there would be the snorting of a feral pig, scampering through the night. Then there would be the whistles and hoots of child gangs in the shadows of nearby streets. These groups of children, many as young as Liam, had deserted their poverty-stricken families or had been abandonded by them. They made their living in the cloak of night, rolling men for pay and robbing shops of anything they could lay hands on.

Mother and Abigail were sleeping, and Liam at last quieted down. According to the mantel clock that Mother kept on a tiny table near her cot, it was nearing midnight. Patrick knew he should be sleeping. It wasn't wise to stay up, knowing that the factory whistle would blow at five in the morning. But as often as he could, he would come out to the steps to breathe the night air, to watch for the sneaky moon, to think. And to write.

Two cats, now visible in a silvery sliver of moonlight, began a brawl beneath the steps. They dove, snarling and hissing, latching onto each other's necks and dissolving into a rolling, tangled mass of fur. Patrick pressed his face between the slats and watched. He'd seen boys act like this many times. Snarling, yelling, fighting over nothing more than a look or a word or a bit of space on the street corner.

Patrick closed his eyes and thought of the Pennsylvania farm. He remembered working up potato hills while Abigail and Mother hung clothes up on the line and Liam tossed a stick to their dog. The soil was rich and red, and smelled fine and earthy.

Worms and grubs wriggled and curled in each shovelful of soil. Sunlight sparkled on the tiny bits of quartz in the dirt. Somewhere in the trees beyond the garden, mockingbirds called to each other. Father came out of the barn, holding a pitchfork, laughing and shaking hay out of his dark hair.

"Patrick, you digging your way clear through the world, boy?" Father said with a wink. "You know, you keep going, you'll either hit the devil or a Chinaman on the head with that spade."

Patrick grinned and said, "I suspect the Chinaman will be a gentleman about it, but not the devil. Maybe I could bribe him with some of those huge trout you caught this morning. That will assure me safe passage, do you think?"

Father chuckled, picked up a handful of soil, and flung it at his son. Patrick ducked in time. The trout Father had caught that morning had been pitifully small things, more like minnows than anything else. They'd joked about those fish for more than a week.

His father said, "You're a bright boy, Patrick. You'll do something fine with your life. I'm proud of you."

Why can't we go back and change things? Patrick thought. *Why must time always go forward and never backward?*

"Patrick Thomas O'Neill, if I see correctly. And what are you doing out late like this? Isn't this past your bedtime?"

Patrick opened his eyes. Down where the cats had been moments earlier stood James Greig, an eighteen-year-old boy with long, scraggly brown hair and clothes that were frayed remnants. He lived no-where, having run off from his family, who lived with other Irish immigrants in the shanty outside of town. James stayed wherever he could find space for a night, a loner, not joining any gangs, more satisfied to be independent. He was wild and loud, and he was Patrick's friend.

"Oh," said Patrick. "I'm enjoying the view from this nice balcony. I'm planning my day tomorrow, which will be full of relaxation and recreation, as are all my Tuesdays."

James grinned, his bright eyes full of mischief. "Aye? And what did you do today, me rich friend?"

"Much the same as I'll do tomorrow," said Patrick, grinning broadly. "Sleep until ten. Dine on quail and cakes. Stroll through the shops up on the high ridge of town and buy whatever catches my attention. You should be jealous of me, James."

James laughed out loud. "Oh, yes, I'm jealous," he said. "Jealous that you work fourteen straight hours a day. Jealous that you don't see the sun except on long summer days and Sundays." James swung around the step beam and climbed the rickety stairs to Patrick. He sat down and raked a strand of hair behind his ear. The boy smelled of smoke and beer. "Jealous that you are always tired and your back aches you. Jealous that there is no future for you in all that, me friend."

Patrick's smile faded. "How can you talk of the future, James? How can you see anything?"

"Oh, easily," said James. He pulled a cigar from the pocket of his tattered brown shirt, struck a sulfur match on the rough wood of the landing, and puffed until smoke came through his lips. The glow circled his face, revealing the scar that ran from his left ear to his forehead. "I take care of meself, you know that. And I took care of you, if I remember correctly. You were attacked by that child gang last year and I rescued you, pulling you out from under just as a knife came at your throat. Anyone who is brave as me has a future, Patrick."

Patrick said, "Perhaps."

"Me future is clear in me mind," James continued. He took out the cigar and blew smoke toward the sky. "I wish you would share the vision. We really are one of a kind, aye, you and me. We're both the bottom of the barrel, both poor old cellar vermin. Looked down on by those with more money, but smarter than the lot of them. We won't be poor forever. I have a vision, and it's a fine one."

Patrick rubbed his chin and sighed. "Your vision. Nothing there but danger, I assure you."

"Aye! Danger and excitement. They go together. When was the last time you had excitement?"

Patrick shrugged.

"Should I guess, then?" said James. "Be it when Liam brought home his first, measly pay? Or when your mother was given permission to salvage the not-quite-wilted flowers from Mrs. Clatterbuck's house to arrange in your own flat in a pickle jar?"

Patrick felt heat rise on his neck. James was making fun of him, but he was right. Excitement was not something that existed in Patrick's life.

"Come with me tonight, Patrick," said James. He put his hand on his friend's shoulder. "You won't have to play a part, just be with us. I've got a new friend named Robbie. A free soul such as myself who approves of my kind of occupation. Come tonight, and you can be the watch. Robbie and me'll find you a gift. What do you say?"

"Where do you plan to go?"

James took the cigar from his mouth and tapped the ash. "Don't know yet. Sometimes we plan it, sometimes not. Theft is more fun that way. But, Paddy, whether we know ahead of time or not, it's always—"

"Exciting," finished Patrick.

"Aye."

There was a clatter in the alley, somewhere in the shadows to the right in front of the stoop to the tenement next door. Snarling followed. It was a dog, after a cat, perhaps, or its own shadow. It was a wild dog, alone and independent, like James.

Patrick looked back at James. "I can't chance it."

"Paddy, Paddy, Paddy." James offered the cigar, but Patrick shook his head. James put it back into his mouth. "You're a boy pretending to be a man. I'm a man pretending to be a boy. Me way's much more fun."

"I have family I have to be concerned with."

James made a snorting sound. "I had family. And as Irish immigrants, they ended up in that damn shanty outside of town. I won't have that, you know." James spit on the steps.

Patrick nodded. He knew. Indeed, as poorly as he and his brother and sister were treated and as little compensation as they received, those who weren't native-born had it even worse. The Irish and the French-Canadians had it worst. They were cheated in the stores, cursed in the streets, and even had their homes razed on occasion for fun. All this reminded Patrick of a book he'd read last year, *Uncle Tom's Cabin*. The book had been written before the war and told about the terrible conditions the blacks had at the hands of their masters in the South.

"Men never lack at finding other men to oppress," Patrick said.

"And so," said James, "I've learned that a man must be after his own concerns or he'll wither and die."

He sounds like Mr. Steele, Patrick thought. He said, "I'm sorry, James. I have to think of Liam, and Abigail, and Mother. If I was caught in trouble, I don't know what they would do. Besides, stealing is wrong."

James tugged the cigar from his mouth and studied it for a moment. Then he flung it out into the air. It flipped end over end as it flew, a tiny, glowing missile soon to die. It dropped into the darkness of the alley and vanished. James looked at Patrick, tipped his head, and grinned. "Don't worry a moment, friend. Maybe someday you'll consent to join us, and until then, I'll just have to convince you by giving you a little trinket or two. Here." He fished into his shirt pocket and pulled out several gumdrops. "Got these at Bronlin's shop. He never noticed."

The gumdrops were pressed into Patrick's hand. They were sticky and lint-covered from James's pocket, but that didn't matter. This was candy, rare and wonderful. Patrick put the drops to his nose and smelled their faint, sweet scents.

"Now." James hopped up, gave a little bow, and

clambered down the steps. When he reached the bottom, he called back up, "I'll be back in a night or two. Think it over. We might be born in different countries, but we're both Erin's sons. Your name gives you away, you know. We should stick together."

Patrick felt his mouth water at the smell of the candy.

"Three's a magic number," said James. "You, Robbie, and me. We could work wonders, I would think!"

Patrick raised his hand to wave, and James was gone, running down the street in the night.

Patrick rolled the drops around in his fingers. He picked up his journal and wrote.

These candies from James are stolen. Picked from the tall glass vase when Mr. Bronlin was busy, probably talking to another customer. I can't eat them.

"Liam would enjoy one," he said softly. "Abigail, as well. I can't think of the last time we had gumdrops."

But they are stolen.

With a heavy sigh, Patrick put the journal down. Then he flung the candy into the alley, where they landed somewhere in the darkness with James's cigar. Then he collected his journal, stretched, and went inside to get some sleep before the factory bell rang its early morning greeting.

❧ 9 ❧

THE LEELAND MILLS bell cut through the air, driving an ax into Patrick's dream of floating down a peaceful river on a wooden barge. His eyes fluttered open to the still dark morning and his hand went to his temple and pressed. Already a headache had begun beneath his skull.

I should have been up a half hour ago! he thought.

He sat up quickly, the fragments of the river dream falling away. Abigail's cot was empty, as was Mother's. Even Liam was out of the bed he shared with Patrick. From the sounds in the kitchen, it was clear that everyone was ready to go off to work but Patrick.

"Why did you let me sleep?" Patrick demanded through the half-open door to the kitchen as he slipped into his trousers. The stifling air of the bedroom had him already bathed in sweat, and he wiped his brow with the back of his hand.

"You won't be late, Patrick," Abigail said over the

rattling of tin plates. "Goodness, you complain over a gift of sleep! I've got a breakfast for you here to carry with you."

Patrick pulled his suspenders up over his shoulders and buttoned them at the waistband of his trousers. He had slept in his shirt and would wear it to work. He pulled on his shoes, ran a comb through his dark hair, briefly touched the loose wall plank in which he kept his hidden college dollars, and went out into the kitchen, where at least a small breeze was stirring though the open window.

Seated at the small table, Liam wolfed down spoonfuls of runny egg. Abigail, wearing the same dress she'd worn the day before, stood at the iron cookstove, scraping egg and a slice of bread into a tin cup. An oil lamp blazed on the edge of the table, chasing away the remnants of night.

"Your drinking cup will have to prove itself as a breakfast plate today, Patrick," she said, smiling as she held it out.

Patrick caught the cup in his hand. "Thank you," he said. "But I wish you'd not let me sleep." Most mornings, with an extra few minutes, Patrick would scribble in his journal. This morning there was no time.

Abigail slipped her shawl over her shoulders as Liam put his dishes into the basin. "And why not? You don't think I know about your late nights out on the steps? Out there in the wee hours, talking to yourself on and on. If I didn't know better, I'd take you for a crazy man and have you sent to an asylum. But I know you're only my brother, with a lot of thoughts locked away and the need to get them out.

And so I thought one morning with ten extra minutes in bed couldn't be harmful."

Patrick said, "Thank you." Picking up the haversack from the counter, he stuck in a half apple, some cheese, some hard bread, and his tin cup. Abigail and Liam already had their noon meals in their pails. Then, on impulse, he went back into the bedroom and stuck his journal inside his shirt. If there was a minute during lunch today, he would write.

Out in the hall, other tenants were shaking off sleep and mumbling to each other. Patrick said, "Good morning" to the Patterson family as they passed on their way to the stairs outside. The Pattersons were a silent lot except for the eldest son, Richard, who always gave Patrick a smile and a pleasantry when they passed each other. "I understand the Boston company has decided to give us all a bonus today!" he said. "All the free lint we can carry to stuff our pillows at home!"

Liam, Patrick, and Abigail followed the Pattersons to the wooden steps and down to the alley. Mill operatives were already filling the narrow road, many spitting thick, fiber-filled phlegm onto the street, most chatting, a few laughing.

"Like horses to the plow," Patrick said to himself. He picked bits of egg and bread from his cup as he walked, putting them in his mouth and trying to savor the taste.

"Patrick, you stepped in horse manure yet again," said Liam. "That's the fourth time this morning. Aren't you looking where you are going?"

"Blast," Patrick said, looking down as he stepped out of the fresh, warm pile. "It's leaked in through the cracked sole of my shoe and is all the way up the cuff of my trousers."

Liam laughed out loud, his blue eyes crinkling. *Thank God Liam is able to hold on to his sense of humor,* Patrick thought.

The sun was rising, bathing the grit in the road with sparkles. The mill workers' feet pounded the bright grit into the air, making those with chronic coughs cough more, making those who rarely coughed go into temporary fits. So many operatives came to work in the mill with reasonably good health. So many left sick or dying, with their lungs destroyed and their energy drained away. Yet every morning they got up and they went to work. Day after day after day.

Abigail said suddenly, "There's Sarah! I best catch up with her. I have a lot to talk about. I'll see you boys later!"

She was off, her skirt whipping and her tin cup bouncing from her apron strings. Patrick watched as she linked up with several other girls, all of whom worked with Abigail and Liam in Spinning Room #4. The girls drew together, bending over and talking with animation, but still moving ahead.

"They're talking about Mr. Lance," said Liam, answering Patrick's unasked question. "The new second hand in our room. The girls think he's handsome, and he's not married. There is talk he has money and would be a good husband."

"A second hand with a lot of money? I can't imagine."

"That's what they say. The girls do their work, but whenever he is around they watch him out of the corners of their eyes. Sometimes they primp and giggle. Maybe he has money. Some people have money tucked away, you know. Polly Bruce says Mr. Lance has a lot of money."

Patrick frowned. "Money alone doesn't make for a good husband."

"Maybe not," said Liam. "But maybe so."

Up ahead, the girls linked arms and moved together to Burris Street. They disappeared around the bakery on the corner.

"I heard Abigail say Mr. Lance seemed dreadfully green," said Liam. "What does that mean?"

Patrick shrugged. "I suppose he is shy around girls. Maybe he doesn't quite know how to talk to them."

"Are you green?"

"Me?" Patrick didn't know how to answer Liam. Certainly there were girls who had caught his attention at the mill, but—like Mr. Lance—Patrick didn't really know how to talk to them, either. There was a girl he'd watched a few times in the mornings on the way to work. She was red-haired and had a happy face. But Patrick never knew what to say to her to get her attention. He was afraid he would sound like a fool.

I suppose I am green at that, he thought.

And then Liam said, "Oh, Patrick! She's there again, looking at us!"

Patrick glanced up and saw once again the old woman, seated at her tenement window, staring down at the street over the heads of the other workers and straight at the O'Neill boys. But Patrick didn't look away.

"Now she's watching us in the morning, too!" Liam whispered urgently. "Patrick, I'm scared of her!"

"Then go on," Patrick told his brother. "Just go on. I want to see what she is all about."

"No, Patrick!" Liam grabbed his arm.

"I'll come after you," said Patrick. He looked at the old woman in her window. Her face, cloaked in shadow, was just as hard to decipher in the early morning. But her fingers rose as he watched, and began their strumming and beckoning.

"Patrick!"

"Just go on, Liam! I'll be with you soon! Go!"

His face contorting, Liam spun on his heel and ran off to the end of the block, sending up divots of dust with each footfall, disappearing in the flow of workers. Patrick licked his lip, caught his breath, then forced his gaze back to the old woman's second-floor window.

Come here, the woman's twitching fingers seemed to say. *Come closer!*

Patrick walked slowly over to the dank-smelling brick wall of the tenement. Taking a deep breath, he called, "What do you want?"

The woman looked down. Her cheeks were sunken and hollow, like deflated bellows. The hands stopped their clutching. It made Patrick think of a spider on its web, pausing and waiting to strike.

"What do you want of us?" Patrick repeated.

The head angled even more, and now the nose was visible. It was sharp and big.

"Leave us alone!" Patrick shouted. "Stop watching us!"

And then, suddenly, with another shift of the head, the eyes were visible. Deep, sunken, black eyes, red-rimmed and rheumy. Wide. Staring down. Unblinking.

Patrick gasped.

But then there was something fluttering down from the window, drifting like an oak leaf on a fall breeze. Patrick watched it as it fell and landed on the toe of his boot.

It was a piece of paper.

A note. A note from the witch woman.

Patrick glanced from the note back to the window. But the old woman was gone.

❧ 10 ❧

"YOU'RE SWEATING MIGHTILY today," said Mr. Steele as he slung another load of folded cotton cloth into a crate and picked up a handful of nails. He hammered the wooden lid down on the crate, pushed it aside, and picked up cloth to fold into another. "You ain't getting a fever, are you, boy?"

Patrick straightened from his own folding and pressed his hand to the small of his back. Around and above them, machines thumped and pounded. "No," he said.

"You're pale," said Mr. Steele.

"I'm fine," said Patrick.

"Good, then," said Mr. Steele, pausing to hawk a thick string of saliva on the floor, then brush at it with his shoe. "We can't be slowing down because you get sick. The river's running strong, the canals all full and fast, and the looms are turning out a lot of cloth. There are orders to fill, boy, and fill them, we must. Farms don't run this country now. Mills do. Machines do. We have to keep up."

"I know."

"The train to ship the cloth will be in soon. It won't wait on sick boys."

"I know." Patrick turned his back on the old man and went back to work: folding, lifting, packing, hammering crates shut, and stacking the crates. He couldn't stop thinking about the note in his pocket.

At lunch he rubbed his aching shoulders, filled his cup with water, then sat on a crate to chew his bread. He had not read the note. Maybe it was better just to tear it up and in this way prove to himself whatever the crazy old woman had to say meant nothing to him.

But he knew he would read it. His curiosity was too great.

Carefully, when Mr. Steele was turned the other way, he reached into his shirt pocket and pulled out the paper. He looked at the folded note. It was hot to the touch, perhaps from the heat of his own body, perhaps from the witch's curse. He opened it slowly.

The handwriting, lovely and fluid, caught Patrick by surprise. Surely a witch would have foul-appearing script. But the words were the most interesting of all:

I have seen you these past days. Walking home with your lovely family from a job at the mill, I surmise. My intent wasn't to frighten you, as I think I may have. You look so much like my son, Andrew, back when he was a mill boy. I'm an old woman at a lack for company. If you would ever have a spare moment, we could visit. Please forgive my forwardness. But you do look so much like Andrew.

Mrs. Randolph Wilson

Patrick's eyebrows drew together in disbelief. He read the note again.

If you would ever have a spare moment, we could visit . . . You do look so much like Andrew.

Patrick whispered, "The witch is inviting you to be her company!"

Please forgive my forwardness.

"She's not a witch," Patrick whispered. "She's just a lonely old woman in a second-floor tenement flat."

"What's that you're reading?" came a voice just over Patrick's head. He glanced up at Mr. Steele, who was wiping meat grease from his lips. Patrick quickly folded the paper and put it into his pocket.

"Nothing of interest," he said.

"Oh, is that so?" asked Mr. Steele. "I saw your eyes go big as bowls. What is it, then, a note of affection from a young lady?"

"It's nothing," said Patrick.

"Or is it a notice of termination? Are you let go from your employment here?"

"No."

"Then is it a petition for a turnout? Are you a rabble-rouser, ready to stop working and strike?"

Patrick felt his face flare red. "It's nothing!" he shouted. "Watch your lunch, Mr. Steele. I see a rat sniffing, ready to drag it away!"

Mr. Steele spun about and looked at his food on the crate. There was no rat, but the point was made.

Mr. Steele, grumbling and rubbing his hand across his bald pate, went back to eating.

Patrick went to a far corner of the room where other men chatted about their families and their aches and had no interest in a boy, and crouched down to write quickly in his journal.

Do I want to go visit an old woman I don't know just because I look like her son? What would I say? How could I explain this to Abigail or Liam? They would think I was insane.

Sometimes I feel like I am going insane. What is there in this mill town to keep me from losing my mind, with the constant work and constant pains in my body? Wouldn't a worker with half a mind be of more use than one with a whole mind? He wouldn't argue or think about problems, but would merely do as he is told.

Am I not at that point already?

At least I can still write.

The bell clanged, the looms and spinning frames upstairs roared into action, and it was time to go back to work.

❧ 11 ❧

September 15, 1870

Tonight Mother came home later than usual. It's Saturday, and tomorrow afternoon there is going to be a birthday party at the Clatterbuck house, where she works. She told us that she had spent the entire day cleaning nooks in the house she had not even known existed. Then she told me I would have to go there to help out during the party.

She said, "Mary Clatterbuck is turning fourteen. The serving boy who usually does the job has been hurt badly in a wagon accident and is unable to help. You'll be the waiter. They'll tell you what should be done. You be there, cleaned and fresh, ready to work at noon."

I wanted to argue, but she looked so weary. And then she leaned over and gave me a hug. It was strange. "We can use the money," she said. "And you'll do fine." Then she got up to heat some soup.

She didn't ask me if I wanted to, she just told me I would do it.

I'd rather spend the day scavenging the stables of Leeland, gathering scattered straw to restuff our mattresses. I'd rather muck out those stables than act as a serving boy!

I have only been to the Clatterbuck house twice, but never inside. I can't imagine the place, and I have a good imagination. Mother has never said anything unflattering about her employers, but I can't help but wonder what these people are truly like. Mr. Clatterbuck is one of the owners of Leeland Mills. I suspect a gruff man who would as soon spit at you as talk to you.

I think I would rather fall headlong in the manure I was mucking than serve there tomorrow.

❧ 12 ❧

IT WAS SUNDAY morning, and Abigail and Liam were out in the alley with other tenants, scrubbing down clothing and bed linens in large washbasins. Many operatives went to church on Sunday mornings; Leeland had no shortage of places of worship. There was a Presbyterian church, a Catholic church, a Unitarian church, and a Friends' meetinghouse. But Lucy excused her brood because she worked at the Clatterbucks' seven days a week and couldn't even go herself.

"Pray without stop," she would tell them. "To God, a heart is a church as much as a building."

"God," Patrick prayed as he walked through town, "let this day go by very quickly."

Patrick knew how to clean cotton, how to doff bobbins, how to shear and fold and pack cloth. But what did serving involve? He didn't have a clue.

The Clatterbuck home was on several acres of land by the river, a half mile east of the mill. Patrick's mother had told him all about the rich family for whom she worked. Their house had been built by the Boston company so George Clatterbuck could always be near the factory to keep a close eye on the goings-on. There were tall oak trees on the lane that passed the house, and shorter lilac and azalea shrubs beneath them. The dirt lane was kept scraped and level, unlike the rutted Charlotte Road. Lucy had told her children that a street washer came down the lane on hot, dusty days, sprinkling it with water from holes in a huge barrel on a wagon. There was a brick walkway leading from the lane to the Clatterbuck house. The picket fence and gate were freshly whitewashed.

Several other ornate, two-story houses shared the lane with the Clatterbuck house, owned by stockholders who could afford luxuries such as ornate fretwork and wicker porch furniture. Patrick's stride slowed as he approached the Clatterbucks'. The two times he'd been here, he had never gone any farther than the gate at the end of the brick walk. Each time he'd come to help his mother carry home castoffs that the lady of the house had given the O'Neills on the last two Christmases. The first time it was an armload of cast-off clothes. The second time the gift had been some dented pots that the cook refused to use, saying she couldn't cook fine food with less-than-fine kitchenware.

I don't want to do this, Patrick thought. *I feel like a fool.*

"I must think of the pay," he mumbled as he crossed the wide road to the walkway and the fenced Clatterbuck yard. "Pay I might be able to skim off to put in the wall with my college money. Pay that will buy some extra pork or chicken for the family."

A small, open-air carriage called a tea cart, drawn by a well-groomed and blinkered horse, rumbled by on the lane. A young couple sat in the cart, arm in arm, the woman in a velvet-trimmed hat and the man in black driving gloves. Patrick watched them go by, but they didn't watch him. They stared straight ahead, intent on their destination.

"I'll bet they're going somewhere where other boys will have to wait on them," muttered Patrick. "I'll bet the waiters smile at them, but they won't have a smile in return. A pleasant expression could be too much of a tip."

"Come on in, then, Patrick!" called Lucy O'Neill from the front porch of the house. Patrick spun around and saw her standing there in the shade, one hand on her hip, the other hand whirling impatiently. "We have much to do and there's no time for woolgathering!"

Patrick came through the gate and latched it back, then trotted up the walkway to the porch. He took the three front steps in a single stride. His mother was in her best clothes, a simple blue frock with a small white collar and scuffed black shoes. She opened the door for her son and then followed him into the front hall. Patrick was suddenly aware of his plain mother against this fancy background. Her gray hair was pinned flat, and her hands were gnarled and dry. Her waist, though not thick, was unshapely. Only rich women could afford corsets.

At first Patrick felt as if he couldn't catch his breath. It was the same sensation he'd had when he'd first set foot inside the Leeland Mills. He had never realized a house could be so crowded with things.

The hall was lined with narrow tables and two spindly coat stands. He and his mother had to walk single file in the hall toward the back and the kitchen, and as he passed the other rooms, he peered in and saw that they, too, were filled. Lamps, tidies, overstuffed chairs, display racks, cabinets, pillows of an array of fabrics and designs, and decorative benches took almost every bit of floor space. Lucy had told her children all about the fancy things here, but Patrick had never envisioned that there would be so much.

In just a moment Patrick and his mother were in the Clatterbuck kitchen with the two cooks and the matron of the house herself.

Mrs. Clatterbuck, a woman not much older than Mother, wore a serious expression on her chubby face. She was dressed for the afternoon party, which would begin in less than an hour. Her hair was swept high, and over her lace dress she wore a white shawl. There were lacy gloves with pearl buttons on her hands.

"So this is your boy, Mrs. O'Neill," Mrs. Clatterbuck said, pursing her lips. "Not really a boy, but nearly a man. I will hope for nothing less from him than a man's effort." She then turned to Patrick, who stood watching the cooks scurry and clamor around him, lifting pot lids and muttering to each other. "The job isn't hard, boy," the matron said. "Look at me!"

Patrick looked.

"There's no counting to do, nothing to read," the woman said sharply. "Just go where you are told and when you are told. Be careful and smile. Nothing is to be spilled. Nothing should even so much as teeter on a tray. Any questions?"

Patrick drove his teeth together and he said, "No questions, ma'am."

"Then I'll be off to greet the company," said Mrs. Clatterbuck. "It is noon. We will settle in the dining room at one, and you will listen for my bell then. This is my little Mary's fourteenth birthday party, and it will be a day to remember."

The cooks said, "Yes, ma'am." Lucy O'Neill said, "Yes, ma'am." Patrick felt his lip twitch as he said, "Yes, ma'am."

At least at the mill, he thought as he was given a white jacket to wear over his clothes, *people know I'm smart. They have seen me writing, and many of them can't even recite their letters. I don't have to play stupid. I do my work, and as long as I do it right, I'm left alone. I don't think I'll be left alone here.*

The kitchen burst into renewed activity. Dishes were set out to go around the dining table in the next room, and Lucy O'Neill quickly hurried them in through a swinging door. As Patrick buttoned his jacket, he tried to see into the dining room before the door swung closed, but couldn't. A cook caught his arm and spun him around to face her.

"You waiting for a proper invitation before you begin your job?" she asked. She was much shorter than Patrick, with a thick neck and arms that seemed full of enough muscle to bind and toss bales of raw cotton at the mill. Her hair was pure white like old cobwebs, combed and pinned against her skull. Her face was red with heat, and her eyes were tiny and keen.

"No, ma'am," Patrick said instinctively.

The second cook, a much younger woman with red hair, laughed as she ladled oysters from a large pan onto a platter. "You don't need to call her ma'am," she said. "We may be chickens with a pecking order in this kitchen, and the eldest can peck the hardest, but only women with enough money to wear gloves indoors require the title ma'am."

"Oh," said Patrick. "All right."

"Until serving time comes, boy," said the white-haired cook, "you will help us here. We have scraps to take out back. We have wood to bring in from the back porch to keep the stove going. And mind, keep that jacket clean."

Patrick thought it was unwise to carry garbage and wood in a white jacket, but he said nothing. He did as he was directed, carrying pans of vegetable scraps and ham fat to the compost pile out back and hauling split wood gingerly in a canvas slip for the two stoves.

On his third trip for wood, Patrick paused to scratch his neck in the backyard, and noticed the whitewashed barn just beyond the fence. He looked back to make sure a cook wasn't watching him from the kitchen window, then carried the armload of wood back to the fence.

The whitewashed barn was actually a five-stall stable. Four stalls appeared empty, but in the fifth, a small brown horse, a pony actually, had its head poking out and its large black eyes staring at Patrick.

"Hey, boy," Patrick said in a clear, quiet voice.

Instantly four more pony faces came to the windows of the four other stalls. Patrick smiled in surprise. "My goodness, you have friends."

Each pony was a different color: a bay, a dun with a large white blaze, a black, a chestnut, and the last one dapple gray. Such an assortment reminded Patrick of the rainbow candy displays in the window of Bronlin's shop on Burris Street.

"She don't care for them any more than she would a piece of dung in a ditch," said a voice nearby. Patrick whipped about to see an old man in dark pants and leather apron standing outside the paddock on a graveled path. He wore a flat hat and no shirt. A heavy leather harness was slung across his shoulder.

"Excuse me?" Patrick said.

The man shifted from one foot to the other; the metal on the harness jingled. "She don't care for them," he said, tipping his head toward the whitewashed stable and the five ponies. "Got 'em for her birthday last year. I heard her begging her father. 'I'll love them, Papa,' she said. 'Five ponies, one for each weekday. My friends and I can have rides, all at the same time. We can have a cart, and take trips up into town to shop!' "

Patrick said, "Who?"

"Why, Mary Clatterbuck," said the man. "George's youngest daughter. The spoiled thing that runs that household as if she was queen."

"Oh."

"She told her father if he got her those ponies for her birthday, she would help me care for them. You see, I'm the man in charge of the animals and the gardening. I ain't got time for five more! But Mary said, 'Oh, Papa, you know I'll help Jed.' That's me, Jed. She said, 'I'll remind him that my ponies need trimming and grooming and their stalls cleaned. I'll help him, too, Papa!' "

Patrick said, "They look healthy."

Jed snorted. He wiped sweat from the bridge of his nose. "You over there where you can't see and can't smell. Those ponies ain't been cleaned in over a week. She forgets, comes out every few weeks and looks 'em over. Never cleans 'em, though. Never feeds 'em except a sugar cube from the kitchen every so often. I swore to myself I wouldn't take care of 'em if she didn't care, but I just can't see them going lame on my account. They got thrush and grease heel, but I don't aim to let them founder. I try to keep up with 'em all."

"That's terrible."

"Mary had her fun for a while, then went off on another curiosity. Never seen a girl so taken with herself and nothing or nobody else. Sometimes I just think I should open the stalls and let 'em all go free."

Patrick nodded.

"You seem like a nice boy," said Jed. "You one of them Irish?"

"Not exactly. We're from Pennsylvania. My mother is a maid here."

"Company's arrived!" It was Lucy, shrieking from the back porch. "Patrick, what on earth is holding you up out there? It's ten till one! Get inside this moment!"

Giving Jed a quick nod, Patrick steadied his grip on the canvas sling handles and hurried across the yard to the porch, then up into the steaming kitchen.

❧ 13 ❧

LUCY BENT OVER Patrick's ear, her words a buzzing, angry whisper. "Don't dawdle. What are you trying to do, have me dismissed?"

"No," said Patrick. He didn't look at his mother. The flurry in the kitchen was about to explode into full-fledged business in which he would be swept up. He put the wood down by a stove and stood straight, flicking a bit of bark from his white jacket.

It did, indeed, look like the party was ready. The table in the center of the kitchen was crowded with dishes of aromatic foods. Beans, potato balls, roasted turkey, and ham baked in cider were ready for the guests. There were also large bowls of spinach, sweet potatoes, boiled rockfish, and several kinds of jellies. Patrick thought about pinching his nose to keep out the wonderful smells so his stomach wouldn't growl, but he knew that wouldn't be polite.

Suddenly the swinging door burst in, and a girl bounced into the kitchen. She was a few years younger than Patrick, with blond hair and bright green eyes. She was dressed in yellow, with a bodice of lace and satin bows in her hair. She wore white buttoned gloves like Mrs. Clatterbuck.

"Oh!" the girl shrieked, her loud voice unbecoming to her appearance. "Look at this! It is fine, I tell you! This is to be such a wonderful party. My friends will be jealous, and will all want such a party on their (sixteenth) fourteenth birthdays, as well. Perhaps, Emily and Lucy and Stella, I should hire you all out to them so they can celebrate in like fashion!"

The two cooks smiled and curtsied slightly. Lucy smiled on cue. Patrick's arms slipped behind his back, and one hand caught the other. He thought it would be best to stand still and not be noticed.

But it wasn't to be so. She noticed him almost immediately, and her head tilted in haughty curiosity. "Well, Emily, I see your Randolph couldn't help us today."

The red-haired cook said, "No, ma'am. He's broken his arm."

The girl crossed her arms and came around the food-bedecked table. "That's a pity," she said, without looking at the cook. But Patrick could hear no pity in her voice whatsoever. As she approached him, he felt an urge to back up.

"And what is your name, boy?" the girl asked.

"Patrick O'Neill," said Patrick. "What's yours?"

The girl's eyes widened, and she drew herself up. Emily and Stella glanced at each other. Lucy's brows pulled together.

"Have you no manners at all, boy?" said the girl. "Where on earth did they find the likes of you?"

Lucy said, "He's my son, ma'am. And I do apologize for his rudeness."

"Let him apologize himself," said the girl.

Patrick felt the words stinging his throat, but they came out in spite of himself. "I apologize."

The girl touched her lips with her finger and let out a disgusted puff of air. "I'm certain you'll remember your place, boy. Speak when spoken to. That will not be too hard to remember, will it?"

"No," said Patrick, thinking that Mary Clatterbuck was just like her mother.

The smile came back over Mary's face, so quickly it was startling. She laughed as though she'd been correcting a dog and was now cheerfully satisfied that the dog had learned the lesson. "Then I'll be off. We'll be ready soon. Listen for the bell and be quick! This will be a most extraordinary party!"

And then she was gone through the swinging door to the dining room from which many new voices drifted. It was to be a big party indeed.

"Patrick!" hissed Lucy. "What is on your mind, son, to speak out to the mistress? I told you last night that you were to be quiet and obedient!"

"But, Mother," began Patrick.

"Hush, now," said Lucy, turning away and snatching a starched towel from a countertop. She began to wash the utensils used to prepare the meal.

Emily walked over to Patrick. "Now, you listen," she said. "You're to be the only one going in and out of the dining room, so I best tell you the order in which the food is taken. The oysters are first, with the sauce, all on this silver tray. You see how well it fits? You hold the tray over their left shoulders, and spoon the oysters onto the plates with this spoon. Offer the sauce, which goes into the small white china bowls. The oysters are slippery things, so mind you don't let one escape into a lady's hair or a gentleman's lap."

Patrick nodded. He knew Emily was trying to make him laugh, or at least smile, but he couldn't.

A few minutes later, the bell rang. Patrick picked up the silver tray with the oysters and pushed through the swinging door into the dining room.

In the center of the room was a huge table covered in white linen and fine dishes. Well-dressed people sat with cloth napkins in their laps, hands folded properly. Mary Clatterbuck sat between two young girls and they giggled as they talked. Across from them was a mustached boy a little older than Patrick, and another girl, about seventeen, with brown hair and a blue dress. No one looked up as Patrick entered, and he felt a certain gratefulness for being an invisible serving boy.

He went around successfully, although his hands were sweating and he could feel the tray trembling just slightly in his grasp. Oysters were served without so much as a stumble. He hurried back into the kitchen for the next instructions.

Emily was testing the doneness of a cake. Stella was slicing fruit and arranging it. Lucy was gone, back to her more maidly duties, Patrick guessed.

"Let's see this," said Emily as she pulled a thin wooden stick from the center of the cake and frowned. "Another ten minutes," she muttered. "It best be done and garnished before the end of the meal or Mary will have a scene."

She glanced over at Patrick, who was unsure what to do next. "Listen for the bell, Patrick," she said. "Then it will be the turkey and ham, which go in the center near the master's chair so he can be in charge of them. You'll serve the potatoes and beans and other side dishes, as quickly and as carefully as you can. The same as it was for the oysters, over the left shoulders."

Patrick said, "I understand."

The next half hour of the meal went well. Every so often he felt the brown-haired girl looking at him, and his ears would go hot. Her name was Nancy, and she was a Clatterbuck, too. The conversation in the dining room was constant yet dignified; Patrick almost laughed out loud thinking how James would react to such civility.

But then it was time to bring in all five of Mary's birthday cakes. The first three cakes came in, a white cake, a chocolate cake, and one with pineapple pieces trimming the edges. Then Patrick went back to the kitchen for the fourth, but when he reentered the dining room, Mary was staring at him.

What does she want? he thought as he placed the coconut-covered cake on the table. *She didn't call me, did she? She didn't ask me a question that I didn't hear, did she?*

Then Mary said, over the hand-muffled giggling of her friends, "You are a mill rat, aren't you?"

Patrick's heart picked up speed. Everyone else in the dining room turned to listen. "What?" he managed to say.

The brown-haired girl said, "Mary, aren't these cakes lovely?"

But Mary ignored her older sister. "Are you deaf from the machinery noises, boy? Didn't you hear my question?" she asked. The girl on Mary's right ducked her head a little bit, obviously pleased with Mary's taunting but deliciously uncomfortable with the scene it was beginning to cause.

The boy across the table from Mary said, "Mary, we'll have that stop now. This is a party, not a competition of wits. I believe we would all have jollification as opposed to idle barbs tossed at a serving boy."

Mary tipped her head and flashed her eyes at the boy. "Listen to me, my dear brother John," she said. "Today the pleasures are mine, and I'll choose them as I see fit. If I want to talk with the serving boy, I'll do so." Mary looked back up at Patrick across the table. "I said, are you a mill rat?"

Patrick said, "I don't understand."

The girls on Mary's sides burst into uncontrollable, shaking giggles. Egged on by their approval, Mary said, "Mill rat. A rat from the mill. A smelly thing that crawls about in the factory, never coming out in the light of day. Eating crumbs in a hurry, scuttling in and out of the looms and spinning frames, getting dirty and not knowing or caring. My father tells me about them. He watches all of you. He tells what happens at the mill to those in Boston who own the majority of the shares."

Mr. Clatterbuck spoke up. "Mary, that isn't fair. People have different stations in life. We've taught you this. We are all equal in the eyes of God."

Mrs. Clatterbuck didn't seem to agree. "This is Mary's birthday," she said. "I won't have it fall apart and be ruined with an argument about your theories on equality."

I see Mary is her mother's daughter, Patrick thought.

Mary was determined to make her point. "Are you a mill rat? Answer me!"

He knew he had to answer, or he would be in trouble. Not only that, his mother would suffer the results. It didn't matter how he answered; it was addressing the question that was the degradation, the acknowledgment that someone could ask him such a thing, and that he had to respond.

"No," he said.

Mary said, "Hmmm. You smell like one. You do stink, you know. Have you no water with which to bathe?"

John said, "Mary, that's plenty from you on the matter."

"Yes, Mary," said Nancy. "Let us be on with our party."

"Hush," said Mary. "I said, boy, have you no water in your home?"

Patrick said nothing, and picked up an empty tray to carry it into the kitchen. Mary hooked her foot out and caught Patrick's ankle and he stumbled, dropping the tray and the remaining potatoes to the floor.

Mrs. Clatterbuck scowled.

Mary said, "Careless mill rat!"

Patrick snatched the tray up as quickly as he could regain his balance, but Mary caught him by the wrist and persisted with her questions.

"I asked you a question. You don't dare ignore me," she said coldly.

Patrick felt his nostrils flare and his wrist burn where she had touched him. He said, "We bring it in."

"Clearly not enough to do the job," Mary said, turning to her friends and giggling.

"Mary," said John, "stop it. Leave him alone. I aim to enjoy myself, and I won't have you making other folks irritable."

"What folks are irritable?" asked Mary. "Just you, Nancy, and Father."

John slammed his napkin on the tabletop. "I am embarrassed that my sister acts like a prissy, snotty child!"

"John!" shouted Mary.

"John!" said Mrs. Clatterbuck. "That is not appropriate. We have guests!"

John stood, throwing his chair back, and stalked from the room. Nancy looked at Patrick and said, "I hope there are more cakes in the kitchen. Please, I'd like to see what other good pastries we have to eat." She gave Patrick a small, apologetic smile, and Patrick went back for the cake.

After dinner, Patrick stayed to help clear the table and collect the garbage to go out of the house. He didn't speak to the cooks or to his mother except to answer questions with as little detail as possible. He was too angry to talk.

"Is this what money can do to people?" he whispered to himself. "I've never seen myself as less than anyone else before. What gives them the right to think they are better?"

He had never been so glad to get out of a place, not even the mill, as he was when he was excused from work at four-thirty that afternoon. Lucy waved him a curt good-bye, and he walked back into town.

But something led him in a different direction than home.

❧ 14 ❧

H E STOPPED ON Charlotte Road, amid the late Sunday afternoon pedestrians, horses, dogs, and rattling wagons. He squinted up at the second-floor window where the witch had sat and had tossed her note.

Don't be silly, go on home, one part of his mind instructed. But something even stronger said, *Visit her.*

He stood another few minutes, his veins still hot with fury, glancing between the tips of his scuffed shoes and the window. Then, before he could talk himself out of it, he took the steps two at a time and went inside the hallway.

For some reason, he had to meet her. It was a test, he supposed. A dare to himself. James dared himself all the time. Patrick sometimes felt like the boy James accused him of being. And today he'd had to be a boy, a sniveling little serving boy, enduring a rich girl's insults.

But not now.

Now he would meet the woman who had frightened his brother and sister. He would prove himself to himself.

It was the first door on the left. He knocked on the splintering wood, peeking over his shoulder in case someone might be there, ready to clock him on the head, believing he had something worth stealing.

I wonder if she has a gun, Patrick thought suddenly with horror. But then it was too late. The flat door creaked open. Patrick stepped out of the hall and into the old woman's home.

For a moment he stood, shocked and awed. Such a difference here from his own tenement flat. Yes, it was tiny, as small as the O'Neills', but there was something that he'd not seen since he'd left the farm back in Pennsylvania many years ago.

There was dignity.

It wasn't so much in the quality of things. The chairs were old, the table scratched and marred. There were dented cooking pots, several iron trivets, chipped teacups. But the difference was in the arrangement, the tidiness, the pride with which the few trinkets had been arranged.

In the center of the floor the old woman stood, her wrinkled hands folded against the bodice of her blue dress, her white hair tied back, her lips tugging in a hesitant smile.

"Hello," said Patrick.

The woman only nodded.

"I read your note," he said, feeling ridiculous, because of course she knew. Why else would he have come?

The woman nodded.

"My name is Patrick. And you're Mrs. Wilson."

The woman nodded. Then she eased herself down on a fabric-covered chair. She pointed to an upright wooden one, indicating Patrick should sit. He hesitated, then sat. *She's feebleminded*, he thought.

The woman was smiling, but Patrick suddenly realized that there was no insanity there. Only appreciation. Her eyes were bright and intelligent.

"Mrs. Wilson," said Patrick, "did you want to talk?"

Mrs. Wilson picked up a tablet from a chair-side stand and began to write with determined strokes. Patrick watched her.

"I thought you wanted to talk to me," Patrick said as the old woman continued to write. Then she leaned over, her back cracking, and handed the note to Patrick. It read, in the same cultured script as the first note:

Thank you for coming. Excuse me that I don't speak. I was working in the Pemberton Mill ten years ago in Lawrence when the mill building collapsed. So many were killed or maimed. My throat was crushed. I didn't die, but was left mute.

Patrick took a breath and looked up at the woman. "I'm sorry."

The woman smiled, then quickly wrote another note and passed it over.

It was a while ago. I get along. My son, Andrew, lives with me here, and my life is full.

"Andrew lives with you? Is he here now?"

The woman shook her head. She pointed out the window.

"He isn't home yet?"

Mrs. Wilson nodded.

"Where does Andrew work?"

Mrs. Wilson pointed at Patrick.

"At the mill? At Leeland Mills?"

Mrs. Wilson nodded.

"Oh," said Patrick. "I see. Is he an overseer or a second hand in one of the rooms?"

Mrs. Wilson wrote and passed the note.

Not anymore. He worked with me at Pemberton, when he was in his teens. He became an overseer at twenty-three. He was a fine one, a fair one. Opinionated, but I wouldn't have had him any other way. But he is no longer an overseer.

"Why not?"

Mrs. Wilson rocked back a little in her chair. She stretched her legs out, and Patrick could see they were in great need of a foot stool. The veins on her lower calves were dark blue and purple. One ankle was swollen with arthritis. She wrote:

He became involved in labor strikes. In turnouts. He detested the conditions at Pemberton. Such danger, such hours, can't be long tolerated. He led a turnout, but it was a failure. No one in charge cared to read his petition or hear his concerns. Not a week after the turnout, the mill collapsed.

Patrick put his elbows on his knees and leaned forward, reading. Mrs. Wilson and her son had certainly been through some hard times. He had tried to do what was right. And she had lost her voice because of the poorly constructed mill.

She gave him another note.

I was so injured I could no longer work. At least I had my legs and arms. Some workers had limbs ripped from their bodies by the falling machines. I'm lucky. I can still think. I can still write, thank God. But with the mill gone, workers had to go elsewhere. Andrew received a bad report from the Pemberton mill owners when he went to look for other work. And so when we came to Leeland the management gave him a low-paying job. He had to accept what they offered.

Patrick said, "I've worked at Leeland for three years now. I've seen bad things, too. When I lived on a farm I had no idea how money could corrupt people. How it could make employers care little or nothing for their workers. But I don't know if I could join a turnout. The owners have the reins, they make money, and we can do nothing except make it for them. I don't want to lose my job."

The woman nodded.

"I'm not much of a fighter," said Patrick.

Mrs. Wilson wrote:

There are many ways to fight, Patrick. I think you would stand up for your values if you had to.

Patrick couldn't answer.

The old woman stood up, put the tablet aside, and

hobbled to the window. She put her hands on the sill and looked out. Loose white hairs caught in an updraft and floated about her face. To anyone in the street below, she would appear to be a witch-woman. Patrick looked around the room, noticing for the first time a silver tea set on a shelf. *I hope James doesn't find out about that,* he thought. *He'd be here in an eye's wink.*

Then she turned back to Patrick. She poured a small cup of coffee from the single-eye cookstove and held it out. Patrick took it and sipped. It was bitter, but not much worse than the O'Neills' usual fare.

"Thank you," he said.

Mrs. Wilson sat and picked up the tablet again. She wrote and passed the paper over.

You have a brother and a sister?

Patrick sipped, then said, "Yes. Abigail and Liam. They work in the mill, too."

You do look like Andrew as a very young man. Except that Andrew had a beard.

"My mother doesn't think a beard is appropriate for me yet," said Patrick. "She still sees me as . . ." He hesitated. "She sees me as still a farm boy. I don't know when she'll understand that I'm nearly seventeen and grown."

What is it you want to do with your life, Patrick? Are you hoping to become an overseer in Leeland Mills?

"It may seem silly, but I want to go to college and be a writer."

How wonderful! There is a new university in New York, called Cornell. It opened two years ago, but this very year they are allowing women to attend. If I was young, I would go there! Writing is such a joy. I would have fancied being a journalist.

Mrs. Wilson went on to explain that she had been raised by educated parents in the South, but because they didn't believe in owning slaves, they weren't able to keep up with the neighboring planters and so lost most of their land. They moved north for a new start. But they never quite got on their feet as they'd hoped. She worked as one of the Lowell mill girls for a while, then was married. After her son was born, she kept on working just to keep the family from going into serious poverty.

But if I wasn't able to give a lot of fine things to my son as I'd had as a child, at least I taught him about the cruelty of owning others or treating them as if they were owned.

"I'm saving up for college," said Patrick, now excited by the conversation. "Our wages are low, and there are many things we have to buy. Also, Mother insists we have a family savings, and we each contribute to it on payday." He leaned over his knees, his fingers linking together. "But I've got nineteen dollars hidden in my bedroom in the wall. It's taken me three years, but I've got that much. It shouldn't be long before I have enough! I don't know what it would cost, but I'm guessing I'm close. Don't you think?"

Mrs. Wilson looked pensive, then she wrote:

The article said the tuition at Cornell is ten dollars a trimester.

"A what?"

That would be thirty dollars a year.

Patrick was shocked. "Thirty dollars a year? How long until I can save even another eleven dollars? All Liam and Abigail make goes to pay rent. My wages as well as Mother's pay for fuel and food. I give money to Mr. Spilman each week so I can have lunch with my sister and brother. And then there's the blasted family savings. Putting away pennies a week is all I can do!"

Mrs. Wilson shrugged and sighed.

"I'll be ninety before I have saved enough, and by then I'll be as senile as a stick!" Patrick stood up.

Mrs. Wilson pointed to Patrick and then to the floor, raising her eyebrows in a question.

"Will I come again?" asked Patrick. "I don't know. I'm busy with work, with my chores at home. I don't know. Thanks for the coffee."

Mrs. Wilson stood up and took Patrick's hand in her own. She squeezed it gently.

Patrick felt a sudden welling of tears in his eyes. His throat went tight. With a quick, nodded thank-you, he opened the door and went out to the step landing. He leaned on the railing, closing his eyes, taking deep breaths of squalid air.

Then, as quickly as one of Leeland's stray dogs, he slipped down to the street and back into the cloak of night.

❧ 15 ❧

September 16, 1870

Ever since we moved to Leeland, I've felt my soul changing. I've worked hard, but to what end? Doing right has never been a choice. It has been the only option. But recently I have felt a shift in my heart, a hardening of my spirit.

I don't like it.

I don't like it, but I don't know how to stop it.

My father said I would do something fine with my life. He said he would be proud of me. I don't think I know how to live up to that anymore.

Nineteen dollars. It's all I have, and it will be quite a long time before it grows to even twenty. What a fool I've been. A foolish dreamer all these years!

I felt sorry for the cooks at the Clatterbuck home at first, but now I think my sorrow was ill spent. These women realize they can't change themselves or their lot in life. Maybe accepting the lot is the only way to remain sane.

James has told me many times that there are two kinds of people. Those who take advantage, and those of whom advantage is taken. He says we are the poor, we are the betrayed. He justifies his stealing this way. He has no dream other than to get what he can while he can.

Me, a writer? What folly that was. I shall be a mill worker for my entire life.

He put his pen down and listened to the night sounds. Tonight, though, he didn't hear children or adults or cats or dogs.

I fancy I hear screaming ponies and screaming people, trapped in wooden buildings, rotting to death as machinery plays their terrible tunes.

Somehow, yet again, I have to get used to it all.

❧ 16 ❧

"SO TELL ME. What was it like in your new profession?" asked James Greig. He had come up the steps and was seated beside Patrick, his fingers wrapped around his knees, the crumbs from a roll he'd just eaten spattering the front of his ragged coat.

Patrick shrugged, putting aside his journal, in which he had just put ideas for a new poem about ponies. "I was a waiter. I waited. I served. I removed rubbish and brought in wood. There was nothing to it."

"Will you quit the mill now, aye? Work full-time there with your mother?"

"No, they only needed me for a day. The usual boy was injured and couldn't work."

James sniffed, his nose twitching. "What are they like?"

"The Clatterbucks? Rich."

"Besides rich."

"Mrs. Clatterbuck and her daughter are intolerable. Rude. Selfish. Cruel. How my mother puts up with it all is beyond me. But she does. We put up with so much, don't we?"

"Not me. I put up with what I want to put up with," said James. He popped his knuckles, then said, "What is it like there, in that house?"

"I suppose it's like any other house belonging to people of means," said Patrick.

"But what exactly was it like? You came in the front door, right? What was there?"

Patrick scowled and scratched his face. "I don't want to think about it. It's over and done with. I waited. They paid me a quarter dollar."

James spat down the steps. "Quarter dollar!"

"I suppose that's fair," said Patrick.

"It's not fair if they could pay more," said James. "Now, think. What was inside the front door?"

"Why do you want to know?"

"Maybe I want to be their waiter someday, who knows?"

"Never," said Patrick, rolling his eyes at his friend.

"Humor me," said James. "Be a storyteller, for goodness' sake. Entertain me. We both know I can't afford to attend the theater or go down to a big city for the trotting races."

Patrick cleared his throat. "All right," he said. "There was a hall in the center. Gas lamps that smelled bad. Hot air from vents. There was a living room and parlor on the left, a dining room and library on the right."

"Details, me man. You ain't much of a storyteller."

Patrick smacked at a fly by his ear. "All right," he

said. "In the hall there was a tall mirror with a gold frame. There was a red runner all the way to the back of the house, and a matching red runner going up the stairs to the second floor."

"Persian runners?"

"I don't know. How would I know?"

"I need to know," said James. "There's an old white-haired rascal I know who pays me for much of what I take, and he then ships the items off elsewhere for sale. He's a crafty old thief, but we get along on the occasions when we do business. He taught me the value of things. Persian runners are the best. Now, have they got a dog?"

"I don't think so. I didn't see a dog. Why?"

"No matter. What else is there?"

"Narrow tables lining the hall, full of gimcracks and such."

"Now you're talking, Patrick. What kind of gimcracks?"

"Every sort you could imagine, and then some you probably couldn't. Figurines, little oil and gas lamps merely for decoration. Big mirrors. Tiny mirrors. Little paintings in frames. So much you could only walk in single file in the hall. And in the parlor, there was an upright piano with tidies lining the top, and vases on top of the tidies and another lamp shaped like a dragon."

James nodded, pulled a gumdrop from his pocket, and offered it to Patrick. Patrick hesitated, then put it in his mouth. "Amazing place, it seems," said James.

"Yes," said Patrick. "All the rooms were so furnished that you could barely turn around. Chairs, tables. I've never seen quite so much excess in one place at one time."

"Country boy." James smiled.

"Perhaps," said Patrick. "But at least we could walk about in our old house without worrying that we would break something for doing so!" He grinned. "And anything we had wasn't worth so much that we'd cry if it did break."

"I wonder if all large houses are decorated in such detail," said James.

"Why do you care?" asked Patrick. "Are you planning on becoming a respectable gentleman now, with a job as a clerk or policeman so you can marry well and buy a house? If so, you best make enough money to hire several cooks and a maid and a waiter on party days."

James said nothing, but the sudden change in his grin cleared up Patrick's confusion.

"James," said Patrick. "James, don't."

"Are you a mind reader as well as a waiter and mill worker, Patrick? Such skills could take you far," James said.

"No, James, you can't," Patrick said.

"What do you mean, Paddy?" James's cheeks twitched with glee. "I can do what I want."

"Please don't go to the Clatterbucks'. Leave them alone."

James stood up and stretched, his arms popping. "Now, Paddy, don't get yourself in a stew. I've honed me trade, and I won't be caught."

"Shh, speak more softly," said Patrick as he looked back over his shoulder, through the open door to where his family slept in the small flat. "It's not about being caught."

James popped another gumdrop into his mouth, chewed it silently, then said, "Aye, it is. It's not wrong if you don't get caught."

It's about Nancy. It's about John. James wouldn't only be taking advantage of the mother and daughter, but of the sister and brother as well. "Leave, James," said Patrick. "I don't want to talk about this anymore."

"Patrick, you know your way around in the house. You could be our eyes, Robbie's and mine. You think they'd miss anything we'd take? You yourself said you had never seen such excess. You yourself said you didn't like them."

"I didn't like what they were like," said Patrick. He remembered the ponies. He remembered the fallen tray, the angry dowager, the sting of fury he'd felt when Mary had said he smelled.

"We won't be long there," said James. "Just a few minutes at the most, but enough time to pick up some valuable items to sell. This, my friend, is something you can do for your mother. An extra income to supplement that pathetic mill pay."

Suddenly the September air seemed very cold indeed. Patrick began to shake.

"Hey, Paddy, we have to do what we have to do. We'll go tomorrow night, around midnight. What do you say?" James's hand came down on Patrick's shoulder, and Patrick was glad he didn't mention the trembling.

"Perhaps," Patrick said finally. "You might have a point."

"Aye! They won't miss a thing, and if they do, it

won't make them starve. It won't throw them into the streets for lack of it. They won't end up in a tenement building with no clean water and no heat, or in a shanty, trying to make a living working in a stinking mill for loss of a few gimcracks."

"Perhaps I will come with you. I don't know. Let me think on it."

James clapped Patrick on the back and said, "Think on it. I'll be off now, Paddy. Tomorrow I'll be by at midnight, and if you're here, the three of us will slip down to the river and the Clatterbucks' fancy house. We'll make it there by one. People are usually well asleep by then."

Patrick nodded, but his neck hurt in doing so. He was still shaking, and it wouldn't ease. "Perhaps."

"You'll be glad you decided to share the vision!" said James as he slipped down the steps and vanished into the night.

"Only time will tell," Patrick whispered to the empty space where James had sat. He rubbed his arms vigorously, trying to rid himself of the trembling before he collected his journal and pen and went in to bed.

17

PATRICK HAD SUGGESTED the three of them eat their noon meal together today, even though it was only Monday. Abigail had questioned it, but Liam had thought it was a fine idea. "Yes," he'd said as they'd walked across the workers' bridge with the other operatives at a quarter to six that morning. "Now we'll eat together on Mondays and Wednesdays."

"No, no, not two days a week," said Patrick. "Not an addition but a trade. Only this week."

"Why?" asked Liam. He picked up a stick and flung it through the bridge railing to the churning river below.

Because I don't know what is going to happen this evening, Patrick thought. *If I go with James to the Clatterbucks' tonight, who knows where I might be come morning?* But he said, "Just tell your Mr. Gilbert that I'll be coming up so he can unlock the door and let me in. He will, won't he?"

Abigail shrugged. The overseer in Spinning Room #4 liked Liam enough to let Patrick into the room on Wednesdays, but this might be too much. "I don't know, but I'll ask," she said.

"Thank you."

Several children raced past the O'Neills on the bridge, squeezing through the knot of adults and vanishing. Liam took off after them.

Abigail and Patrick walked together. Then Abigail said, "Patrick, you seem to have a lot on your mind."

"I always have a lot on my mind."

"But more than usual. I know you get up at night and go outside. Tell me, are you meeting a girl?"

"No!"

"Then you are writing a book, aren't you? You've always wanted to. You are writing a book and you are going to sell it for a lot of money. You just don't want to say anything yet. Am I right? You'll write a book and make so much money we won't have to work in the blasted mill any longer."

Patrick found himself almost smiling. Abigail believed he could do something with his writing. "Sure," he lied. "That's what I'm doing. But don't you tell anyone. It's a secret until it's done."

Abigail said, "I won't! That's wonderful, Patrick. I'd do anything to get out of the mill, and maybe this will be our answer."

They stepped off the bridge and passed through the gates of the mill yard, bumping along in the sea of workers. Before them and on both sides, the brick buildings of the complex stretched. In the center of the yard, Abigail would go right to climb the stairs to the spinning floor, and Patrick would go left, then around the building to the storage room next to the train tracks.

"Ask your overseer about today," Patrick reminded his sister as they parted.

The storage room was beginning to hum with activity. New crates that were stacked outside in the yard had to be brought inside and placed in rows. Men grumbled, stretching in preparation for the long day.

Patrick dipped his tin cup into the bucket of water for a quick sip before starting. Last night, in his bed, he'd calculated that he would need to save over one hundred more dollars if he was to go to college. He'd written:

I might as well dream of being the king of England. Today and every day from now on, work will be only that. Not for the future, but for the brain-numbing present. Food, rent, food, rent. A cycle of minimums, nothing more. I'm a horse walking circles, grinding my life away. I can't feel anything anymore. This is the worst day of my life, except for the day that Father died.

Patrick tossed the rest of the water onto the floor. Mr. Steele wiped his face with a dirty handkerchief and said, "Morning."

Patrick nodded in response, and then the first loads of cotton cloth came in on the carts and the day began.

18

PATRICK, ABIGAIL, AND Liam sat together for their noon dinner break in the filthy aisle next to Abigail's spinning frames. Mr. Spilman had agreed, to the dismay of Mr. Depper, to let Patrick trade a day for a day. And Liam had coaxed his own overseer, Mr. Gilbert, to unlock the doors when Patrick had pounded from outside on the stairs.

The spinning room was very large, filled with the long machines that made spools of thread from the coarser cotton fibers. When running, the machines had to be tended carefully; broken threads had to be tied and full spools replaced with empty ones in the blink of an eye. Windows were never opened, because the air needed to be warm and damp to prevent frequent thread breakage. If the room wasn't humid enough, it was sprayed down with water.

Making fabric wasn't a complex process, but it was backbreaking and tedious. The raw cotton came in on the trains, was combed free of tangles, dirt, and other impurities on the dreaded toothed carding machines, spun into thread on spools on the spinning machines, then woven on looms, cut, and packed for shipment. There was not a job within these walls that was without danger from bad air, vicious machines, or too much noise.

Seated all around the O'Neills were the workers who kept the spinning machines running and who took off full spools and put empty ones on. The operatives were primarily women because this job offered lower pay. Men, most people believed, were heads of their families and therefore should get better-paying jobs. The spinners talked among themselves and munched on whatever they'd packed in their pails. A good number of them paused to dip snuff from apron pockets. They claimed it helped reduce the irritating effects of lint in their throats.

Liam had dumped his pail out onto his lap, while both Abigail and Patrick ate one piece at a time out of their own pails.

"So tell us truly, Patrick," Abigail asked. "Why did you prefer Monday to Wednesday for our dinner together?"

He shrugged. It wasn't something he could explain. He took a bite of his pear half and couldn't taste it at all.

"You make no sense," she said.

"True. I don't."

"You keep making changes and they will stop our family lunches altogether. You know we can only do it because Mr. Gilbert has a liking for Liam. Others resent us at times and have said so."

"It's just this week. I promise." He could promise that, truly. Because if he was caught stealing, he'd never eat another lunch with his brother and sister in the mill. He'd be eating in the town jail, or worse.

Liam thumped Patrick on the arm. "You aren't eating your dinner." He leaned over and tickled Patrick in the ribs, hoping for a laugh. Patrick knew this, and forced himself to grin. "I'm all right, little brother," Patrick said. "Just hot and tired is all. The bundling has been especially furious these past weeks, what with the new looms upstairs and the river being so high and fast. I've got a third more to do in the same time, it seems."

Liam said, "They should hire another boy or girl for doffing and oiling. I've got two machines to attend. Two of those long, blasted things! It used to be easier, but now my head spins, just like the bobbins, so fast I can hardly see. I've been kicked twice today for not moving quickly enough."

"I'm sorry," said Patrick.

Then Abigail said, "Oh, there is Mr. Lance!"

Patrick swiped sweat from his eyes and watched the man as he strolled about, watching over his charges.

He was younger than most of the overseers and second hands at the mill, in his midtwenties at the most. He seemed energetic, with neatly combed blond hair and a trim mustache. His clothes, although coated with lint, were in good repair and of good quality. But it was clear he was none too happy to be in the noisy mill. He strode boldly as though he were only passing through.

"I don't know him," said Patrick. "Many second

hands move up from other jobs, but I've never seen him before, and I've worked all over this place. How long has he been here?"

"About six months," said Abigail.

"And where did he come from?" asked Patrick.

"I'm not sure," said Abigail. "Sarah says he must be the son of a stockholder, with those clothes. Isn't he fine?"

"Why would a stockholder's son work as a second hand? That's beneath his station."

"I don't know and I don't care," said Abigail. She touched her face and rose up on her knees a little. "He isn't married."

"What importance is that?"

Abigail turned a furious eye on her younger brother. "Don't be naive. And I won't say more in front of Liam."

"Abigail, you know nothing about this man. He kicked your little brother."

"I know, and I'm sorry for that. But Liam does tend to dawdle, if you haven't noticed. And Mr. Lance didn't really kick hard."

"He kicked hard," said Liam.

"Would you two just be quiet?" said Abigail. "You don't know anything!"

"Don't make a spectacle," said Patrick. "And don't do anything foolish."

Abigail pushed loose hairs back from her face. Her mouth was set with resolve. "I'll do what I have to do," she said.

Mr. Lance passed them, staring straight ahead. Abigail's gaze followed him for a moment. She said, "Eat your meal, Patrick. You've only got a few minutes before the break is over. I won't have you here any longer, trying to spoil my chances." Her eyes twitched and her mouth set in a straight line.

"He kicked our brother," Patrick said. But Abigail ignored him.

Patrick pretended to chew his food, but he couldn't swallow it, and when time came to go out, he spit most of it back into his pail.

❧ 19 ❧

STEPPING OFF THE bridge onto Burris Street, Patrick wiped rainwater from his eyes and said, "Go on home without me tonight. I've got something to do."

Liam's nose wrinkled. "Like what? It's raining. What have you got to do in the rain?"

"I know it's raining. Just go on."

"But why?" asked Abigail.

"It doesn't matter. Just do this for me, all right?"

"I don't understand," said Abigail.

Frustrated, Patrick drew his fists up in his pockets. "You don't have to understand everything I do, do you? Can't I ever have time to do anything by myself? I just need time by myself. Is that so odd?"

Abigail stared at Patrick a moment, then took Liam by the arm. "Fine, then," she said. "You go right ahead. Don't melt."

His brother and sister strode up Burris as Patrick moved over and waited under the lip of the supply store's roof. He watched workers come in and out of the store. The red-haired girl he thought was cute came out with her father, and he turned his head and dipped his chin into the collar of his coat, hoping she wouldn't recognize him tonight.

When his sister and brother were out of sight, he walked back out to the road. An old man, digging through a pile of rubbish beside a shop door, looked up at him, water coursing from the brim of his battered hat, and said, "You got something for me, boy?"

Patrick said, "Nothing, you worthless bum." The cruel words stung his lips, but he held on to the burn to punish himself. He walked up Burris, gaslights humming in the growing darkness, passing the closed shops and men who were coming out of shop doors, locking them and double-checking them because there were always thieves wanting to help themselves. He headed for Charlotte Road.

Mrs. Wilson had wanted him to visit again. "Why not tonight?" he mumbled to himself. "Maybe she can talk me out of going with James."

He quickly climbed her steps and tapped on her door. He tipped his head and listened. "Mrs. Wilson?" he called. A little girl, farther down the hall in near darkness, said, "Hey, mister, where you going?"

Patrick sneered and said, "Go home, little girl. There are dangerous men about!"

She squealed and ran into her flat, slamming the door.

Now I'm talking like this to children, Patrick thought. *What is wrong with me?* "Mrs. Wilson?"

The door opened, and he went inside.

She was wearing a pale pink dress, old but attractive. She smiled broadly and touched his arm in tentative yet friendly greeting. Motioning to the wooden chair for Patrick, she sat opposite. The room smelled good, like cooked apples. The cookstove was scrubbed, the wooden floor had been washed. Clean bowls and plates lined the shelf, and beside them, the silver tea set gleamed.

Mrs. Wilson handed a note to Patrick.

So glad you came back! I love visitors. How was your day at the mill?

Patrick looked up from the paper. He said, "The same. It's always the same." He wanted to tell her of his despair, but was hoping, instead, that she would read it in his tone, in his face. "Work is hard. I don't think the world will ever run out of cotton for cloth."

Mrs. Wilson leaned back her head as if to chuckle. She wrote:

You may be right. And people will always want more cloth, so work is steady. That's good.

Patrick felt like balling this note up. Instead, he put it on his leg. Rainwater dripped from his clothes to her floor, making small puddles. "It's not so good. Our wages are lower now than they were a year ago. So many people are needing jobs now. We Yankees. The immigrants, flooding in, wanting work. Competition is fierce for those jobs. The immigrants have been willing to work for less pay, so the mill owners have brought the wage levels down for us all. Everyone loses, Mrs. Wilson. Everyone, that is, except the stockholders." He paused and blew out an angry breath. "Everyone except people like the Clatterbucks."

Mrs. Wilson wasn't smiling now. She had folded her hands across her lap, and her head was tilted. She nodded, sighed, then lifted her pen again.

You not only look like my Andrew, but you sound like he used to sound. He saw how bad things could be when we worked back at Pemberton. He often said, "The rich men line their pockets with gold. But they should make it fairly, with fibers and not with our blood." Andrew had many listening to him. I loved to hear him as much as anyone. Then he led the turnout and found the company to be stronger than he was.

Patrick read the note. He said, "I may feel like that, but as I've said, I can't see myself going out on strike. I'm not that brave."

As I've said, there are different ways of fighting. Different kinds of bravery. You came up here to visit me, and you didn't even know me. You may well have thought me to be a crazy woman, but you came. You are brave. And as a writer, you can be a powerful fighter. Words have strength of their own.

Patrick looked away from the woman. Surely she must be able to see that he was nothing special.

I believe you have a good heart. You'll follow it.

Patrick looked at the floor. He hesitated, then said, "Mrs. Wilson . . ."

And then the door was shoved open, and a man came into the tiny room. He was tall and pale with a large, bent nose. When he swiped his hat from his head, his bald head reflected the lamplight.

"Mr. Steele!" said Patrick.

The man frowned and pushed the door closed with his foot, looking from the old woman to Patrick. He said, "Mother, what is this boy doing here?"

Mrs. Wilson began to write, but Patrick stood quickly, notes fluttering to the floor. He stammered, "I came to visit. She invited me."

Mr. Steele tossed his hat onto the small table. His face flushed red, more red than Patrick could ever remember, even on the hottest summer days in the storage room. "How's that? She can't speak! Are you checking on me, boy?"

"No!"

"Have the supervisors paid you to spy on me, to find a reason to let me go? Has my past so stained me that I'll not be wanted anywhere? There's nothing I've instigated in Leeland. I have never even encouraged men to turn out, you know that!"

"I know that, Mr. Steele," said Patrick. "Wait, please."

Mrs. Wilson stood from her chair and jammed a note into her son's hand. He read it, stammered, then shook his head. He walked to the window and, much as his mother often did, put his hands on the sill and gazed down into the street. Only there were very few hairs stirred by the breeze.

Patrick's heart was hammering. Mr. Steele was a

rabble-rouser? This bald, thin, coughing man didn't have a leader's bone in his body!

Mrs. Wilson scribbled a quick note and gave it to Patrick.

Will you stay for dinner?

Patrick shook his head. "No, thank you." He'd wanted to hear her words of wisdom, but there was no way he could talk candidly with Mr. Steele in the room. Maybe fate had played this hand for him. He waved at Mrs. Wilson, then left the flat.

At home, on the steps, he wrote,

People change. Mr. Steele changed. I've changed. I know the truth about myself now. I'm a mill rat. It's time I understood and accepted that.

He kicked a road stone and sent it flying.

I'm just a mill rat. So be it.

❧ 20 ❧

PATRICK, HOLD STILL. I can't pin this if you keep pacing round the kitchen!"

Abigail sat at the kitchen table, straight pins in her hand. Her face was pinched in a frustrated scowl. Patrick, sighing, wandered back from the window. "Sorry."

Abigail grabbed his sleeve once more and said, "This isn't going to take but a minute. You just have to make your feet stay put. I have to let the cuffs down in that shirt. You look like a scarecrow with such long arms."

"Scarecrow!" chuckled Liam, who was in the bedroom with the door open, an oil lantern on the floor at his feet. He was cleaning the family's shoes with a rag, trying to keep the leather from cracking any more than it already had.

Patrick tried to stand still with his arms out as Abigail adjusted the freed hems of the sleeves. He knew they wouldn't be long enough even if she let them out to the very ends, because it was a shirt he'd had for two years, and his arms had grown like vines.

"We'll have to use some of our family savings to buy cotton cloth for a new shirt for you soon," said Abigail in resignation. "It can't be helped."

"I suppose," said Patrick. "The mill should give us some as bonus, but that will never happen, will it?" In the flat next door, something slammed the wall. A rough voice yelled something, and a woman began to cry.

"So," called Liam. "You really talked to the witch? You really scolded her, and told her she best leave us be?"

For the tenth time since he'd come home, Patrick said, "Yes, Liam. She cowered at my words and slunk back into her flat. She'll never gawk at us again."

"That's wonderful!"

"I suppose it is," Patrick said. He had thought of telling his sister and brother the truth about Mrs. Wilson, but the idea of their seeing him as a hero was too strong. He was desperate for them to think highly of him tonight; their awestruck admiration was like a strong, if temporary, tonic. The truth of the old woman would have been an empty victory.

There was another thump on the wall, and another shout.

"I wish the Pattersons would quiet down at night," said Liam. "They yell so much. Maybe they would be nicer if they just got some rest."

"Hush and clean those shoes," said Abigail. "We haven't got time to worry about Pattersons. Patrick, hold still!"

Patrick again tried to plant his feet and make

them behave. But nervousness thrummed through his muscles like the waves on the river. Tonight Robbie and James were going to the Clatterbucks' house to rob them. What would Mother say if she knew?

A moment later, after some tugging and *tsk*ing, Abigail said, "There. Done. Take the shirt off and I'll stitch the hems up."

Patrick slipped out of his shirt and gave it to his sister. He said, "If we were as rich as the people Mother works for, you wouldn't have to take such care with such a poor excuse for a shirt, trying to make it into something it doesn't want to be."

"Wouldn't that be something!" said Liam. "Polly Bruce says her uncle, who lives in Baltimore, is so rich he has a tailor to make different shirts for each day of the week! Seven shirts, can you see that?"

"My," said Abigail. She threaded a needle, holding it close to the light of the kitchen's lamp, and slipped a knot into the thread's end. "To be so wealthy! Mother could have a fine house with a porch, and she could sit and knit all day if she wished. Or take a nap."

Liam came into the kitchen and put the shoes on the table. "I'll be an overseer one day, and will make enough money to buy Mother a nice house by the river."

Patrick looked at his brother's nine fingers but said nothing.

"I'll be out of the mill in a year, maybe less," said Abigail. She held one shirt cuff up close and ran the thread in and out, securing the raw end of the material. "Just you wait."

"How is that?" asked Liam.

Patrick went to the kitchen window and looked out at the wooden steps and the black, callous night. "Answer your little brother, Abigail," he said, looking around.

"Oh," his sister said. "I have my plans." She gave Patrick a furious look but said no more on the matter.

The wall between the O'Neills and the Pattersons was slammed again, and the man began yelling. His voice rambled on and on, rising in pitch and going down again.

"They have to be quiet," said Abigail, her voice pinched with irritation. "We need to get some sleep soon."

Patrick walked over to the wall and put his ear against it. "That's rude," said Abigail, but Patrick flicked his hand at her.

Patrick couldn't hear the words, but the emotion was instantly clear. This wasn't the usual Patterson argument; something was wrong. Both Mr. and Mrs. Patterson were crying, yelling, pleading.

"Patrick, get away from that wall this moment," said Abigail. "Have you no manners at all?"

Liam said, "Patrick, stop it."

"Shhh," he said. He pushed his ear harder against the wood, causing it to sting. He could hear footsteps, pacing. Then Mrs. Patterson was against the wall, and her agonized words were finally clear.

Patrick listened, swallowing hard, then moved away and dropped into a kitchen chair.

"What?" asked Abigail.

Patrick put his forehead down on his arms. He could smell his own skin, feel the light tickle of the hairs. Surprisingly, tears came to his eyes, and he rubbed them away.

"Patrick, what is it?" demanded Abigail.

"It will never stop. We're locked in, like forgotten ponies."

"What are you talking about?"

"Their son was crippled today. Richard Patterson. His legs were cut off," Patrick said, his head not lifting, his words buffeted against the skin on his arms. "Richard. The only one of the family to ever give us a smile. I liked him."

Abigail shook her head.

Patrick spat, "Are you surprised? Should any of us be surprised? What have we learned these years in the mills, Abigail? That hard work will make our lives better? I think not!"

"You're scaring me, Patrick," said Liam.

Abigail said, "We have to take something to them. Mother would be angry if we didn't take bread, something. We should be good neighbors in this terrible time!"

"You visit them, Abigail!" Patrick shouted, his head going up, his eyes locking with his sister's. "We have our own matters to attend to. We can't save the world!"

"What's wrong with you? What is making you talk like this?"

"Nothing," Patrick said. "Nothing. I'm just wonderful." He stormed out of the flat and sat on the steps to wait for midnight and for James. He would go tonight. It was decided. His arms itched as though someone were tickling them with feathers.

Lucy came home, climbing the flights of wooden

steps with slow, steady footsteps. She frowned when she saw Patrick on the landing, but he assured her he was fine and just wanted a little time alone. He didn't tell her about Richard Patterson. Abigail would do that. A half hour or so later, he heard no more sounds in the O'Neill flat, and knew they had all gone to bed.

Across the alley, in other brick tenements, other families were sleeping. Only rare and occasional lights could be seen from windows. The air was scented with another impending rain, and the sky was a pewter cloud, heavy and threatening thunder and lightning.

Storm's coming, Patrick thought. He crossed his arms and put his chin on them. *Storm is on the way.*

"Pssst!"

Patrick glanced down. James, in a dark, tattered overcoat, broad-brimmed black hat, and scarf, stood gazing upward. The overcoat and hat looked much like Union issue from the war. This startled Patrick for a moment. His father had worn a hat and coat just like that. Where would James have found old uniforms?

Beside James was another form in dark clothes, head down. Both had burlap bags tucked over their arms.

"You coming?"

Patrick nodded.

"Good, then. Let's be off! We must have this done before the rain. I don't care to trade a chill for a dollar."

Patrick took a deep breath, then slipped down to the alley. He had no coat to wear. He suddenly wished he'd put on the wool shirt, or the jacket he wore in winter. Not because he was so cold, but because covering would give him more of a sense of secrecy. It would cover his exposed nerves and calm him.

"You're shivering," said James.

"No, I'm not," said Patrick.

"Nervous?"

"Should I be?"

James grinned, then put his hand on the shoulder of the person with him. He turned the person around so Patrick could see the face. "Here's me Robbie. Robbie, this is me best friend, Patrick Thomas O'Neill."

Patrick gasped audibly. Robbie, dressed in trousers and coat and cap, was a girl.

❧ 21 ❧

"Now, Paddy, I can't see why you're worried," said James, lighting a cigar as the three crept down side streets, moving toward the lane along the river. "Does it make a difference to you whether a thief be a boy or a girl?"

Patrick hadn't looked at Robbie—or Roberta, as James had explained—since they'd left Patrick's alley. He had his hands shoved into his trouser pockets, heavily. His suspenders cut into his shoulders, but he didn't care.

"Paddy," said James. "I asked you a question."

"It matters," said Patrick.

"Why?"

They reached an intersection, and James peeked around the corner first before waving them on. They hurried across the open space and into another narrow road. There was only another quarter mile until they reached their target.

"Patrick," hissed James, blowing out a thick puff of smoke. "I asked you why."

"I don't know," said Patrick. Robbie walked beside him quietly, with a soft tread.

"It's all right for a man to be crooked, then, and not a woman?"

"I suppose so."

"A woman should be virtuous, Paddy?"

"My mother and my sister work hard for their money."

"Robbie works hard for her money, too," said James. He drew on the cigar and grunted hoarsely. "Her mother worked hard, and she died for it. Came down with consumption because of that damned mill. Left Robbie alone, so where was she to go? She worked the mill for a while, then something happened and she was discharged. Either thievery or prostitution. Not much of a choice, eh?"

Suddenly a strong female voice said, "James, you needn't tell him anything. He doesn't care, and I don't waste breath on those that don't care."

"Aye, Robbie, don't worry. He's good stock, he is. Irish from a ways back, like us," said James. "He cares."

"Don't think so," said Robbie. She looked directly at Patrick then, and he at her. Her eyebrows drew a distrustful line across her shadowed face. Her eyes, which sparkled golden brown in the faint haze from a distant streetlight, narrowed and twitched. "He don't live in the Grove, does he, out in the shanties with the others? He don't have our way of talking. He sounds like a native-born to me."

"He is native-born," said James. "I told you that. But he's a fair shake."

Robbie took a deep, loud breath, then turned her attention forward. She shifted her burlap bag from one arm to the other.

James dropped his cigar to the road and pressed the smoldering tip out with his shoe. He said, "She was a worker at Leeland. Spent her time in a carding room, and you know how hard that work is. Those machincs'll cat you up and spit you out."

Like Liam, thought Patrick. *Like Richard Patterson.*

Robbie swore and kicked at a rock on the road.

"But being such a pretty girl," James went on, "it was too much for a new second hand, and he took advantage."

Patrick stopped in his tracks. "What are you saying?"

"She's got a bairn on the way now," said James.

"A . . . ?"

"Bairn, Paddy. A child."

Patrick looked from James to Robbie. Both stared at him, looking so much alike in their clothes, only Robbie's face thinner and more drawn, and James's face covered with several days' unshaven growth.

"A second hand?" asked Patrick. "And now there's going to be a bastard child?"

Suddenly James was on Patrick, his fist in Patrick's stomach, his other hand wrapped tightly about Patrick's neck. Patrick gasped and tried to pull free.

"Don't you ever say that about me, Robbie!" James snarled. "There's no bastard!"

"James, stop it!" Patrick managed.

"There's no bastard! Robbie's me wife, Patrick!"

"What?" Patrick struggled, trying to get away.

James gave a shove, sending Patrick to the ground. "I said she's me wife!"

James stepped back, blowing angry breaths and slamming his fists one in the other, as though he was trying hard not to strike Patrick again. "Aye, you heard right. I found her one night a month ago, dismissed from Leeland Mill for un-Christian character. Un-Christian!" James spat the word out as if it was foul to his mouth. "The second hand violates her, makes her a mother before her time, before she is even fifteen, and they deem her a bad lot! She was curled up under some stairs, by rubbish piles, fighting not to cry."

"I didn't cry," said Robbie.

"I know you didn't cry, you fought hard," said James. Then to Patrick he said, "If I was a mill worker at that moment, I'd have called to my fellow operatives for a turnout. I'd have beat the man, then shouted and caused as much trouble for the mill as possible. But as it is, I'm only a street urchin. I had nothing to offer this girl."

"It's getting late," said Robbie. "We best get down to that house and get our job done." She walked off, leaving James and Patrick behind.

"And you've married this girl?" asked Patrick.

"Well, married in me mind and in hers," said James softly now. "We's as good as married. We stick together now." He sighed. Then he smiled a wan smile. "Never could see me as a husband, could you, Patrick?"

Patrick said, "No."

"Enough dallying," James said. "Gimcracks waiting. Ah, glimmering, gilt-edged gimcracks!"

"Yes."

The boys trotted quietly down the road and caught up with Robbie, who was quite a ways ahead.

❧ 22 ❧

THE CLATTERBUCK HOUSE, standing tall and foreboding in its fence-enclosed yard, was dark. No lights were visible. The family had retired for the night.

Robbie, Patrick, and James stood out on the lane, huddled at the base of an oak tree, watching for any signs that might indicate someone inside was still up and moving about. The other large houses along the lane were dark, too, and only a single dog, deep within the confines of one home, barked a string of muffled complaints. Overhead, thunder rumbled, but no rain fell.

The Clatterbuck house was silent. Still. And sleeping. James tapped Patrick on the arm. "We'll lead on in, Paddy. I ain't asking you to take anything this go-round. Just you remind us where you saw the best trinkets, and if there is anything we might stumble over in the dark."

"I don't remember that well," said Patrick.

"Sure you do. It'll be a lark, this trip out. And you be at the ready at the door when time comes to leave."

"How do we get inside?"

"We check doors, then windows," said James. "Bound to be something loose or ill shut. Have a knife to pry a loose latch if need be. We'll be in and out and have time to celebrate before the old sun even has an inkling to come up and shine."

"There's many a slip between a cup and a lip," said Patrick.

"But the nectar's sweet once it's in the mouth," answered James. "Here." He pulled the scarf from around his neck and handed it to Patrick. "Your face is as white as a fish belly. Wrap your head and stay low."

Patrick nodded. James pulled his collar up and then ran out from the tree, planting his hand on top of the waist-high fence and hurtling it with the skill of a deer. Robbie followed, hopping the fence just as easily. Patrick tied the scarf around his head as he would have tied a bandage for a toothache, then scurried after. His leaping of the fence wasn't as graceful as the other two, but he made it on the first bound, and felt quite proud.

But his heart thundered painfully.

The grass inside the yard was shorter than that outside it by the lane. Clearly Jed, the gardener and livestock man, had trimmed it in the last few days. The grass trimmed. And what of the ponies and their hooves?

"Psst, come on," James called in a whisper. He and Robbie were already up on the front porch. Patrick followed, stepping lightly, hoping there was no squeaking board or loose nail to trip them up and give them away.

"We'll try this window first," said James, moving behind a tall potted fern and touching the sill. "Best to go through a window if possible. They don't have to open as much, and let in less air and less sound. You stay low with Robbie there, and I'll give it a try. If it goes up, Robbie will go first, then me, then you. Now, what might I find below this window inside?"

Patrick shook his head. "I don't know."

"Shake your head," said Robbie. "You must remember. James said you knew this house."

Patrick tried to think. The room was a study, full of many bookshelves and vases and chairs. But what was where?

"Think, Paddy," said James. He pushed his palms against the window. The glass wouldn't budge. He tugged the knife from his pocket and picked at the seam. Still it wouldn't move.

"Locked," he said. "And no latch I can pick." He climbed out from behind the fern, his face set in new determination.

The window on the other side of the porch was locked as well, tight and secure with not a loose space to be jimmied.

"But look," said Robbie, who was standing at the front door. "The wood here is flaking. See by the knob? Carve it a bit, and I'll get a finger in to flick the latch over."

"Good," said James. Patrick stood back, feeling helpless and frightened, as James began to whittle away chunks of wood from the space by the knob.

Patrick flushed cold, then hot. This delay was making the whole escapade unbearable.

But then James whispered, "Aye, Robbie, those little fingers are better used here than in some blasted mill!"

The door was swinging open, and with blessed silence. Someone had oiled the hinges. Lucy O'Neill, possibly. "She does her job well," Patrick said softly to himself.

The three crept inside the dark, cluttered hallway. They stopped a few feet from the door, and James reached back for Patrick's hand. He leaned around Robbie and muttered, "Where are the best items?"

There were items all over, many of value, Patrick was certain, but which ones would bring the most cash on sale? He couldn't know. So he pointed to the left, into the parlor where the piano stood with the dragon lamp. "Be careful," he whispered, his voice sounding in his ears like trumpeting calls. "There are things everywhere that can be knocked over."

James and Robbie nodded. They moved slowly into the room on the left. Patrick stood by the door, ready to pull it open when it was time to get away.

There was silence, then a soft tapping and clinking sound as James and Robbie picked up trinkets and slipped them into pockets and into the burlap bags. Patrick stared ahead at the staircase. Up those steps his mother's employers slept, unaware of the intruders.

From the parlor came airy murmurs of appreciation. Patrick was struck with a bizarre sense of pride beneath his fear. Pride that he'd brought James to a house with things good enough to put his friend at awe.

And then there was a thumping upstairs.

Patrick's jaw dropped open, his blood stopped in his veins. *No!* He looked into the parlor, at the shadowy figures of James and Robbie, afraid to speak to tell them of the sound, terrified not to.

"Ah, beautiful," James said softly.

Patrick took several steps forward, his gaze locked on the grayness at the top of the stairs. Maybe it was only the creaking house, settling on its foundation. He skirted a hall table and put his hand on the bottom of the banister, tilted his head, and squinted to see farther. There were no lights up there, no visible movement.

"And this is for you," whispered James. "I have chosen something special for you, me friend!"

Robbie said, "That should hold us. Let's be out of here."

There was another creaking sound, this time accompanied by a flash of light. A lamp. Someone was awake upstairs!

"James!" hissed Patrick.

The light up the stairs seemed to explode into full brightness. There was a man's shout, a woman's gasp.

"James!" It was a cry now, because there were shadows in the light at the top of the stairs, shadows moving quickly, feet hitting the landing and then the steps.

There was a crash in the parlor as James and Robbie scrambled, trying to get around the chairs and trinket shelves and out to the hall.

"Hold the door!" James screamed.

Patrick stumbled backward, feeling frantically for the door, watching the couple descending the stairs.

"Halt!" shouted George Clatterbuck. "Halt or I'll shoot!"

"Run!" cried Patrick.

Then Robbie and James were beside him, around him, past him, racing out the door and into the night. Patrick slammed into the doorframe, still staring at the man and woman and the gun, which was now leveled in his direction.

"Halt!"

Patrick backed through the front door just as a bullet whizzed past his ear. Mrs. Clatterbuck screamed.

"Run, James!" Patrick shouted.

The man was faster than the woman. He leapt down the stairs two at a time, dressing coat flapping like a giant bird's wing. "Stop or I'll stop you dead!"

Spinning around, Patrick jumped off the porch onto the walkway. His ankle twisted beneath him as he hit, and he went down on his knees on the brick. That instant he was pushing himself upward, the palms of his hands ripped raw, shoving himself back to his feet. He teetered with the stabbing pain in his ankle, but the bullet that zipped over his head was enough incentive to ignore the pain. He ran down the walkway, into the shadows that were his only salvation.

Two more bullets, in quick succession, flew by.

He reached the fence and cleared it by a foot, but landed on the bad ankle with all his weight and cried out with the agony. Glancing back, he saw Mr. Clatterbuck on the porch, reloading his revolver, while his wife stood, silhouetted behind him, her hands wringing one inside the other. And then light from an upstairs window caught Patrick's gaze, and he looked up.

There was a girl there, his age, looking down into the yard, holding a candle to the glass.

It was Nancy, the oldest daughter. Nancy, who had taken Patrick's part at the cursed birthday party. Patrick swiped sweat from his eyes and stared. *Can she see me?* He could see Nancy in the candle glow, the mouth open slightly in surprise or fear, the hand against the closed window glass.

I'm sorry, Nancy, Patrick thought. *I didn't mean this against you.*

"Halt, thieves!" Mr. Clatterbuck aimed the revolver again, and Patrick ducked, missing a bullet. He scrambled up, wheezing, panting, his hands stupidly grabbing for air to pull him forward.

And then he had his balance.

He ran.

He had no idea where Robbie and James were at this moment, but it didn't matter. He raced along the lane, his ankle complaining with each step, away from the rich homes and the river, up toward the belly of the town where there would be buildings and street corners around which to hide. His lungs ached; his temples throbbed with the panic.

I want to go home!

He reached the end of the lane and darted into an alley behind a row of shops.

I'm safe! I'll make it home!

And then someone jumped out from behind an

empty wagon and tackled him, bringing him down hard, face in the stone and dirt.

"Ugh!" Patrick groaned as his jaw hit ground and sent a fire flash of pain up through his skull.

"You said my name!" It was James, screaming in his ear.

"Get off me!"

James turned Patrick over and straddled him, his hand clamped around Patrick's throat. Patrick twisted violently, trying to shake James off, but the boy clung tightly. "You said my name, you imbecile! You want me found? You want me hanged?"

Patrick slammed his fist into James's chest, and James grunted but didn't let go.

"James. . . . !" Patrick managed.

"Curse you!" James hit him in the head, the chest, the arms, each blow like a crack of steel against Patrick's body.

And then there was someone else beside James, taking his arm and yanking him sideways. His grip loosened on Patrick's throat. Patrick began to cough, clutching at his neck and rolling from beneath James, stopping with his face in the dirt of the road. There was Robbie's higher-pitched voice saying, "James, leave off him. He didn't do nothing wrong."

Patrick ached all over. His ankle, his lungs, and now his arms, chest, and throat. He knew he'd be bruised mightily by morning. And he wouldn't be surprised if something was broken.

"Patrick." It was Robbie, standing over him now. "Patrick, can you turn over?"

Patrick worked his elbows against the rough

ground. There was grit in his mouth and his eyes. He spit. Then he gingerly turned himself over and looked up at Robbie.

"James didn't mean to be so hard," she said. Her dark hat was off her head now. He could see she had fine, blond hair that was pulled back in a braid. "He didn't mean to hurt you."

It felt like he did, Patrick thought.

"But you shouldn't have said my name!" James stood by Robbie now, bending over slightly, staring at Patrick on the ground. "Paddy, you were so careless!"

Robbie looked at James. "There are hundreds of Jameses," she said. "I don't think you'll be found for a single name."

"Maybe," said James. "Maybe not."

Patrick forced himself to sit up. He touched his ankle, his arms. Nothing seemed broken, but they hurt dreadfully. He stood, sucking air through his teeth.

"No one seems to be after us," Patrick said. "We're safe."

James scowled, kicking at the alley dirt, swearing silently to himself. Then he said, "I'm sorry, Paddy. I just . . ." His voice trailed.

Patrick stood as straight as he could. "Yes, I know," he said to James.

Then James burst into uncontrollable laughter. He bent over, clutching his knees. "What a poor shot Mr. Clatterbuck turned out to be!" he said. "How many bullets were there? And not a one striking the target! He must have been on the rebel side during the war!"

Patrick was surprised to hear himself beginning to laugh, too. "I'll bet he was. I'll bet he killed himself a lot of trees and fences with that revolver of his!"

The boys laughed, long and hard, while Robbie stood by silently. And then, when the chuckling eased, she said, "I don't think he were such a poor aim, James."

James said, "What?"

Patrick's smile faded. He frowned at Robbie.

"He got me arm, James. I'm hit." She held up her left arm and tugged back the baggy sleeves of her coat and blouse. It was too dark in the alley to see red, but there was blood there on the skin, black and wet as tar.

"Gone clean through," she said. "In and out. I'm bleeding pretty bad."

James went to Robbie, catching her arm in his hands and pressing the wound. Robbie gasped, but didn't cry out. "Why didn't you say something before now?" asked James. His voice had changed; it was pinched with dread. "Robbie, why didn't you tell me right off?"

"We needed to get away," Robbie said.

"But you're hurt bad!"

"James, we needed to get away. Now we can tend to this." She sucked air with the pain. "I'll be all right."

"Give me the scarf!" James said. Patrick quickly unwound the scarf from his head and tossed it over. James wrapped it about the wound and drew it in tightly, tying the ends.

"You should see a doctor," Patrick said.

"No doctor works for free, Paddy," said James.

"And you think we can give trinkets for cash and not be traced to the crime?"

Patrick stood helplessly as James finished the makeshift bandage, then held Robbie in a clumsy, distraught embrace. After a moment, James collected the burlap bags they'd dropped in the alley, and fished around inside. He pulled out the dragon lamp that had been on the Clatterbucks' piano.

"This is for you, for your trouble," he said. "Take it and sell it. It'll make tonight worth your while."

Patrick didn't know what he was going to say until the words were tumbling out of his mouth. "I don't want it, James."

"Take the thing, Paddy."

"This is blood money, too. Like the mill's profit. Robbie's as wounded as a mill worker would be if she was struck by a flying shuttle on a loom. I won't have it."

James slammed the lamp back into the bag and collected both of them. He slipped his free hand gently around Robbie's waist, then said, "Suit yourself. I haven't time to argue. I've got to find a safe place for Robbie."

Patrick nodded numbly.

"When Robbie's resting tomorrow, what say we do the tobacco shop on Forsyth? I've not tried them, but tobacco is a dandy to many men, and I would think there are coins aplenty in such a shop."

"You want to keep on, after what's happened to Robbie?"

It was Robbie who answered, angrily. "You keep to your business, boy, and we'll keep to ours. I'm fine, and James is here for me."

"The Clatterbucks deserve to be robbed for the robbing they do of their workers," said James. "And the others, the shops and stores? Do you think any of them cares a whit for them that slaves away in the mills? "They do not! Why, it's the mills that owns the stores, and its the mill that sets the prices. So you tell me, Patrick, who's robbing who?" Then James turned, and he and Robbie limped down the alley and out of sight.

The Union cap had fallen to the road, and Patrick picked it up and held it in his hands. He put his face to the rough material and shut his eyes for a moment.

"James is wrong," he whispered.

The he opened his eyes again. "He's wrong!" he shouted to anyone, to no one. His voice echoed, and several distant dogs barked in response, kindred spirits of the night and the desolation.

❧ 23 ❧

September 18, 1870

   Today at the mill there were rumblings about Richard Patterson's amputations. I heard men talking in whispers during the lunch break that enough was enough.

   I pretended I didn't hear their talk, but I listened closely. The term "turnout" was on nearly all their lips. They want to strike tomorrow. I wonder what will happen if they do. There have been other strikes, but most of them small, and workers only ended up reprimanded or let go. But this seems to have the whole mill talking. Even Liam said there was quiet talk in the spinning room, and I heard the dock men chatter about it on our way home.

   As I sit here on the steps, I am wearing the Union cap that James lost. It feels strange yet good on my head. What a silly comfort. Maybe I'm crazy like James, only I don't know it yet!

   Maybe James is right. I wonder what the justice is

of men dying in a war to free the slaves, just so they can become slaves to the mills.

But it doesn't seem right what James is doing. Thieving isn't the answer. I know Polly Bruce told the truth about one thing. There is gold out west. There is money for the taking if someone could get there.

I'm tired.

I can hardly see the stars tonight at all. Everything seems so far away. The stars. Dreams. Everything.

❧ 24 ❧

"THERE'S TALK OF a turnout on behalf of Richard Patterson," said Mr. Steele early Wednesday
afternoon as he slammed a load of folded cloth into
a crate. "Heard mutterings on my way to the mill
this morning."

"I haven't heard a thing," said Patrick around a
mouthful of nails.

"Well, now you have," said Mr. Steele. He pinched
his nose and sniffed, then coughed out onto the
floor. "Now you've heard from me. What're you going to do about it?"

Patrick hammered a nail into the corner of a crate
lid, then moved to the next corner. He spit a nail
into his hand and hammered this corner, too. Then
he said, "Why should I do anything about it?" ·

"You know Richard. He was a bale breaker, and
so were you before you moved here to packing. You
must have worked with him for more than a year."

"Working together doesn't mean intimate acquaintance," said Patrick. He drove the final nail in and hoisted the crate onto a flat, wheeled dolly, then pulled an empty one from his stack and reached for more sheared cloth to fold.

"Didn't say intimate acquaintance," said Mr. Steele. He coughed onto the floor. It was hard to see in the dim, dusty light, but the phlegm seemed to have a red tint to it. "Just said you knew him. And a man crippled is a sorry thing."

Patrick sighed and scratched his forehead with the tip of his hammer. "I know him."

"Live near him, too, don't you?"

"All right, I live near him. Next door to him, in fact. What do you want me to say?"

Mr. Steele coughed, wiped his mouth, and glanced about the huge room, where packers were doing identical work: folding, packing, hammering. Other men pushed loaded handcarts out through the packing room door to the train tracks, where the crates were going into boxcars. Mr. Depper was talking with a packer not too far away, but well beyond hearing range considering the scraping of crates and the overhead pounding of the looms.

"I want you to say," said Mr. Steele, "that my mother hasn't tried to talk you into anything. She admired me once, but no longer. I want you to say you'll stay here with me and those who have sense about them."

"Your mother is a smart woman. She didn't try to talk me into anything. I'm not going out. Richard Patterson was a fool for stumbling in front of a train car."

"Good for you," said Mr. Steele. "That's sensible.

You strike and they'll look at me, too, working next to you and all. I can't have them thinking I'm not loyal."

The afternoon dragged on. The train took off with the fabric, heading for distant destinations.

But suddenly the sounds of the machines stopped. It was as if they had all died suddenly, without warning.

It was four o'clock. The set time.

"They're going out!" a packer shouted.

"Blast!" said Mr. Steele.

Patrick watched as some of the men crowded to the open door. He saw Mr. Depper, appearing from behind a stack of crates, his hands clenching.

"You men get back to your stations!" shouted Mr. Depper. "There is no need or concern outside for you!"

More men went to the door, some of them shouting now, pushing, angry and loud. They huddled together, heads whipping back and forth as if deciding to make a break for it. As if deciding whether Richard Patterson was incentive enough to go out the door, around the building, and join the others who protested mill conditions that could lead to such a crippling. The voices were those of old men, teenagers, middle-aged men. Some high, some low, some growling, some yelling. Through the stacks of crates and bundles of cloth Patrick could make out single words, echoing back.

"Death trap!"

"Inhuman!"

"Unify!"

The men glanced out at the sunlit train yard and

then back into the shadows, struggling with their decision. Mr. Depper was wringing his hands now, clearly taken aback. Mr. Spilman was out of the room, so it was Mr. Depper's task to go into the mob alone.

"Back to work, the whole of you!" he said. He hurried forward into the thickest pack of men, his chubby fists raised now, fleshy clubs that would have no impact, Patrick knew, if the men chose to go. "Don't do this! It will mean your jobs!"

"It might save our lives!" shouted someone in the mob.

Mr. Steele whispered, "Fools. The mill is stronger than we are. How does a rat stand up against a cat?"

Several men in the bunch broke and ran outside, calling back, "Let's all go! There's strength in numbers!" They were cheered on by the others, although some of those cheering were obviously not brave enough to follow.

Mr. Depper, wringing his hands, shouted, "You'll be sorry!"

"Strength in numbers," Patrick said softly. He'd never heard that saying before. "Strength in numbers," he repeated.

"They'll be sorry," said Mr. Steele.

"But if everyone goes, then who is sorry but the owners?" said Patrick. "They can't replace every operative, can they?"

Mr. Steele grabbed Patrick by the arm and drew him up close. Patrick had never seen the old man so furious. "Be quiet! We must save our jobs!"

Patrick looked at Mr. Steele, then back to the door, where only a third of the men had gone out to join the protest. Mr. Steele was right. Not every-one was going, and so those who did were fools.

"I'll be quiet," Patrick said. Mr. Steele let him go, and Patrick went back to fold cloth into yet another crate.

❧ 25 ❧

"THE TURNOUT WAS turned back so quickly," said Liam as the O'Neills walked home that night. "It was loud at first, with people leaving their frames and shouting, but only a few went out."

The night hung heavy; there were no stars, only the tainted yellow of heavy clouds, threatening rain. The Merrimack reflected the yellow, seeming to turn the world on its head.

"A lot of our men went out," said Patrick. "What happened after that, do you know?"

Abigail lifted her skirt slightly as they stepped from the bridge and down to the road. "The striking operatives didn't get far, I heard. They gathered in the front yard, yelling and demanding all mill machinery be turned off until there could be talk between operatives and owners. But the overseers got the clerks from the counting room and they all blocked the bridge. The workers would have rushed them, except the Leeland police showed up. They were threatened with arrest. They were told they would never work in another mill if they took this course. That cooled them down, and it was over."

"Our men were back in twenty minutes," said Patrick. "Was anyone hurt?"

"I don't think so," said Abigail.

"I wanted to go out with them," said Liam. "Only Abigail wouldn't let me."

"You, Liam? A striker?" asked Patrick.

"Richard Patterson was hurt. It could have been you, Patrick. Or me."

"Yes, but . . ." Patrick had nothing else to say. The matter was done and over. Not to be thought of again. They walked another minute. Raindrops began to fall, at first slow, irregular plops, then heavier, rhythmic drips. Today they were going to the market before they went home; because of the operatives' late hours at the mill, farm folk would stay until dark with their wagons, waiting to make a few last sales. Patrick had in his pocket a little money with which to buy whatever vegetables were available, and to pick up a small bag of flour so Abigail could bake tonight.

"Strength in numbers," Patrick muttered, remembering the packer's shout.

"What?" asked Liam.

Patrick shook his head. "Nothing. It was nothing at all."

"Blast," said Abigail. She looked up, put her hands over her head, then lowered them. "If I should only be able to afford a parasol for rain. My hair will be a fright by the time I get home."

"At least it's not snow or sleet," said Liam. "It's not so cold."

Abigail smiled at her little brother and put her arm around him. "Optimist!" she laughed.

The market was one street over from Burris, at a wide intersection of laid brick. Much of the brick was ground down and shattered from wagon wheels and animal hooves, but it was still a busy gathering place for the poorer citizens of Leeland. As the rain continued its steady drone, Patrick bought cornmeal and wheat flour while Abigail and Liam chose beans, corn, and spinach. Patrick paid for each selection, then the family walked back to Burris and up to Charlotte. Then the downpour came.

Abigail shrieked and Liam laughed, and the three held their sacks over their heads as they raced to their tenement building. Patrick didn't even glance up as they passed Mrs. Wilson's window.

Lucy was home already, and was quite irritable. She was suffering with sniffles and a sore throat, and had reluctantly come home early when Mary Clatterbuck had complained of the maid's constant sneezing. Abigail was subsequently irritable, as well, used to being the only woman in the flat until at least eleven, having to defer all her housekeeping decisions to her mother.

"That coffee can be saved," Lucy said as Abigail prepared to take leftover, days-old brew out to dump from the steps. "We can't afford to waste, Abigail."

Abigail clenched her jaw and looked at Patrick for support, but Patrick was seated at the table, one hand caught up in his hair, the other under his chin, unable to care much about the women's disagreement.

"Mother, this is foul," Abigail said. "It's just a taste, and if I leave it in the pot, it will make the coffee tomorrow taste nasty."

"Bring it back," said Lucy. "We won't waste."

Abigail brought the coffee back in. A few minutes later, Lucy stood over Abigail as she mended her stockings. "That seam is crooked," she told her daughter. "You don't want to be seen with uneven seams."

"I don't really care, Mother," said Abigail. "No one sees beneath my skirts but me."

"If you don't take care of small things," said Lucy, sneezing and dabbing at her nose with a dingy handkerchief, "then how can you be trusted with larger things? Rip out that seam and start over."

Abigail snorted, driving her heel down on the floor hard enough to make the floor shake, but she ripped out the seam and began again.

The clock on the mantel read 9:45. It was a good night to go to bed early. Liam bid his family good night and playfully tossed a sock at Patrick, but when Patrick didn't toss it back, he went into the bedroom and dropped onto the bed.

"What is wrong with you?" said Lucy, tiring, finally, of correcting Abigail and ready to straighten out someone else. "You have barely said three words since you came in."

"Tired," said Patrick.

"So am I, but I have the common courtesy to be civil to my family."

"I'm civil. Just tired. Too tired to talk."

"You're upset," said Lucy. "You have no right to be upset, Patrick. Did you know the Clatterbucks were robbed last evening? So much of what they had in the parlor gone! If anyone has a right to be upset, it is they. Now, what's the matter?"

"Nothing," he said.

"I heard there was a turnout at Leeland Mills today," pressed Lucy. "Were you involved? Is that why you are upset?"

Patrick stood up, slamming his chair over, his fingers drawing up into claws. "I wouldn't waste my time on a turnout!" he said. "And I'm not upset! Leave me alone!" He stormed through the doorway and into the dark bedroom. He stripped off his trousers and suspenders and shoes, then climbed into bed beside his brother. His pulse raced, his temples pounded. He took the Union cap from under his pillow and pressed it to his cheek.

"Patrick," said Liam. "Tell me a funny story. Please." The boy's voice was gentle, expectant. If there was any betrayal at all in Patrick's new self, it was in failing Liam.

"I don't have a story to tell," said Patrick. "I'm sorry."

"That's all right," said Liam. "Good night." He patted Patrick on the back, then rolled over with a sigh.

And sometime later, over the quiet arguments of Abigail and their mother, Patrick surrendered to sleep.

❧ 26 ❧

A HAND CAME down on Patrick's mouth, and he awoke with a terror-filled start.

"Don't move, idiot," came a whispered voice. "You'll wake your brother."

Patrick sat up, pushing the hand from his mouth. The voice said, "Be quiet, Paddy!"

James?

Patrick squinted at the form in the darkness. He stopped fighting, and the hand came away. "James," he whispered, "how did you get in here?"

He watched as James left the bedroom for the kitchen. Patrick stood, shaking fogginess from his mind and lifting the cover back onto his sleeping brother, and went out with James. He glanced at the mantel clock. It was 2:35 in the morning.

"I don't believe this," he mumbled to himself.

James stood at the door. "To the landing," he said, whirling his hand for Patrick to come after.

The boys went out to the landing. They stood in

silence, James staring out across the alley, Patrick scratching his head and trying to guess what would make James break into a friend's house. The air smelled of the recent rain.

Finally James said, "So you think I can get into shops and stores but can't manage the door on a tenement flat? I'm disappointed in your lack of confidence."

Patrick stretched his shoulders. "What is this about?"

James said, "I'm going back, Patrick. You may go with me if you'd like."

"Back? Back where?"

"To the Clatterbucks'. I'm going again. Tonight. I didn't take enough from them to make up for what they took from me."

Patrick stared at his friend with his mouth open. "Clatterbucks'? Why, James? You can't. They have a gun and you know they sleep lightly!"

"I don't want them to sleep lightly. I'm going to take a few more things, then I'm going to announce meself. I'm going to tell them what they did. I'm going to shout it from their hallway before I leave. Hah! I hate them! They need to know what they did, Paddy."

Patrick pushed a strand of hair from his forehead. "I don't understand you."

"Robbie," said James. "She lost her baby."

"She what?"

James ripped at a fingernail with his teeth, then spit it out. "Lost it. All the running, the injury in her arm. Gone, Paddy. Early this morning, as we was sleeping in the shed behind the Unitarian church, she went into fits, and not an hour later, the child was out and dead. Me Robbie never screamed, she just held my hands and her breath. I know, though, that she was in bad pain. And so, what I thought was to be my family is gone. Half of me true family struck down and gone."

"The child wasn't yours," said Patrick.

"Its spirit was mine," said James. "Robbie told me so from the beginning. Since I cared about it, its spirit was mine."

"I'm sorry."

"Sorry doesn't change anything. Robbie's so weak now. I have to do something. Something! Someone has to pay, Patrick!" James paused, turned his head away from Patrick, and Patrick was sure the boy was crying. But James would never let Patrick see such a thing. After a few moments, he dragged his hand viciously across his cheeks and chin and looked back. "Going back, Patrick. You come with me?"

"I'm afraid."

"And I ain't?"

"James, the real culprit is the man who violated Robbie. Not the Clatterbucks for protecting their home."

James nodded. "Aye, and I'd kill this bloody Mr. Lance if I could, but I don't know who he is. Where he lives, what he look's like. Robbie refused to tell me. And I ain't about to go poking around the mill to find out. Not yet anyway. But I will. And then there will be hell to pay. You can be bloody well certain of that, me friend."

"James, are you speaking of Mr. Lance who is now second hand in Spinning Room Four?"

"I reckon that must be the one. Why do you ask? Are you saying you know him?"

He shook his head. "No," he lied.

"Come with me, Patrick?"

"No," said Patrick, trying to wave James off. "I have to get some sleep." He felt dazed.

"Didn't think you would," said James. "Is there anything, then, you'd like me to pick up for you?"

Patrick stood, rubbed his arms, and said, "Free the ponies."

"The what?"

The ponies, Patrick thought. But then he said, "Nothing, James. Just my sleepy mind rambling."

James tipped his head, confused. But he said nothing.

And then Patrick went back into the tenement.

27

LUCY WAS NO better the next morning, although she was up with the rest of her family before the mill bell rang, drinking her coffee, preparing to go to the Clatterbucks'.

"They'll only send you home," said Abigail.

"They'll think I've forgotten myself," said Lucy as she stood at the tiny kitchen window, gazing out at nothing. "I can't just not show up."

"They know you're not well; they sent you home last night. Mother, go back to bed and sleep a day. You'll be the better for it tomorrow."

"I know myself, Abigail," said Lucy. "I'm going."

And the four of them went out of the flat, passing the Pattersons in the hall and mumbling an awkward greeting, then down to the alley to head off in their own directions.

As they crossed the covered bridge and Liam found some friends with whom to walk, Patrick said, "Abigail, wait. I need to ask you something important. What do you know of Mr. Lance?"

Abigail blushed and said, "He has money. Shy around ladies, but that's not to be taken as a fault. I think he'll like me if he notices me, Patrick. He just has to notice."

"Keep away from him."

Abigail stopped and frowned. Several mill operatives, walking behind her, bumped into her and then moved around, grumbling. "What business is it of yours?"

"He's not so inexperienced as you might think. He's not a nice man."

Abigail threw back her head and giggled. Her pinned hair threatened to shake loose. "Patrick, I miss Father, too. But you don't need to take his place!"

Patrick caught his sister by both arms and drew his face in close to hers. "Abigail, I'm not trying to father you. I'm trying to protect you."

Abigail's laughter slowed, then vanished. "Let me go. I can't be late to spin and you can't be late to pack."

"We won't be late if you let me say what I have to say. It's only one request. Stay away from Mr. Lance."

Abigail's face darkened, her eyes bright like taunting moons. "What do you want me to be, Patrick? What do you want me to do? Stay as I am now, a little mill girl at her frames, running back and forth day after day, on my feet year after year, with nothing more than that to entice me into my womanhood? I'll have more than you and Liam and Mother, and I'll do what I must to have it!"

"Abigail!" He grabbed for her then, as if holding

on to her would keep her safe and out of harm's way, as if it would protect her from all the dangers of the mill, of Leeland, of the world. But Abigail pulled back just as hard, and with a flip of the head, she spun around and vanished into the flow of operatives.

Patrick watched after her, then looked down at the river. To jump into it now, to wash away like a random stick or leaf, to ride on currents to places unknown. To be free. It would be the easiest way out. He sighed, and it hurt his chest. He jammed his hands into his pockets, finding the Union cap in the right one. It was warm like a glove.

Patrick thought, *Maybe James doesn't know who Mr. Lance is, but I do. I'm forewarned. I know about the man, who he is, what he looks like. I must protect Abigail!*

Work was fast and nonstop, although for a packer to complain to almost anyone else in the mill would be considered an insult. This work didn't take fingers off or crush bones or bring as many workers down with consumption. Beside him, Mr. Steele grumbled occasionally, but Patrick was a master at blocking out what he didn't want to hear. The morning hours lumbered on.

Right before noon, a packer came by Patrick and Mr. Steele and in a quick and subtle motion pulled a folded paper from his shirt and dropped it on the floor. "Read with care," he said as he moved by, looking straight ahead. Patrick watched as the man moved on down the line of packers, dropping papers as he went.

"What is that?" Mr. Steele asked, but Patrick was

faster than he in snatching it from the floor and opening it.

It was one typeset page, a tiny newspaper. *The Workers' Voice.*

Mr. Steele, looking over Patrick's shoulder, said, "Throw that away! We'll be in certain trouble for even looking at it!"

Patrick read the headline of the first article. 'TURNOUT TURNED BACK; WORKERS DECRY MUTILA-TION OF DOCKWORKERS!'

That the paper was out so quickly indicated it had been done locally. And it was sympathetic to the workers.

Mr. Steele grabbed at the paper. Just before he caught hold of it, Patrick was able to see at the bottom a request: "Writers needed."

"Writers needed," Patrick said to himself as Mr. Steele tore the paper into tiny bits and tossed them away.

It was Thursday, so Patrick was supposed to eat in the packing room. But he would go up to talk to Abigail no matter what. She needed to hear the truth about Mr. Lancc. He went to the door, but it was locked as he'd thought it would be. Mr. Depper saw him and called, "Get to your lunch, boy!"

"I need to go upstairs," Patrick said.

Mr. Depper came up to Patrick. He waved his thick index finger and said, "You are going no-where."

Patrick eyed the keys on Mr. Depper's belt loop. "I have to, sir," he said. "It's life or death."

A number of packers nearby heard this and stopped eating. They walked closer, listening, watching. Patrick recognized these men as some who had gone on yesterday's turnout.

Mr. Depper laughed out loud. "Life or death? Really?"

"Please unlock the door."

Mr. Depper said, "I won't repeat myself! Go back to your station."

Patrick hesitated. He looked at the packers, hoping they would follow his lead. He said, "All right, then." He took a step forward, then stumbled into Mr. Depper, pulling the fat man down to the floor with a grunt.

Suddenly the packers were all around them and over them, lifting Mr. Depper up and brushing him off, asking if he was all right. They moved their bodies to block Patrick, so he was able to take the keys he'd tugged from the man's waistband and quickly unlock the door. Then he brought the keys to Mr. Depper.

"Here," he said, handing them over. "These dropped to the floor."

Mr. Depper scowled, took the keys, and tied them back to his belt loop. "Now back to your station, boy. And the rest of you men, return to lunch!"

The men went back. Several gave Patrick a knowing wink. And as soon as Mr. Depper was on his way to the other side of the room, Patrick opened the door quietly and escaped.

He raced up the wooden stairs to the third floor. He waited by the door until a child came out with a cart of fluff, then slipped in. He found his sister and brother in their usual spots on the floor in the aisle.

"Hello!" said Liam. "What are you doing up here today?"

"Patrick?" said Abigail.

"I must talk to you, Abigail. We must talk now."

"Really?" she said. "I don't have time to talk to you. I'm busy."

"Busy eating?"

"Yes," she said, rolling her eyes. "And other things you don't care to hear about."

Patrick could see Mr. Lance now. He was coming their way, although he was not looking at them. On his face was a greasy smile. It made Patrick's stomach turn.

"Patrick, guess what," asked Liam. "Polly Bruce's grandmother was a queen in Europe; did you know that?"

"Be quiet a moment, Liam," said Patrick. Abigail ran her hands through her hair, causing it to ripple down around her shoulders.

"A queen!" said Liam. "I think it would be just fine to go visit her in Europe. Polly said when she's sixteen she'll pay for all of us to go with her and—"

Patrick had reached his limit. He turned on his brother. "Why do you believe that girl and all her lies? Are you so likely to be led around by the nose, taking for truth everything you hear? She's got no money. Her family is poor like we are."

Abigail tossed her head a little, then patted her temples as if she was straightening loose strands to pin them back.

"Patrick, that's mean," said Liam.

"It's not mean, it's real. Now, be quiet!"

Liam's cheeks puffed and his eyes grew tight.

"Be a man," Patrick said.

"I'm not a man," said Liam.

"You might as well be. You're in a man's world." Then he said, "Abigail, listen to me. I have news about your Mr. Lance, and it's not good. Hear me out. It's for your own good."

Abigail ignored Patrick. She called to her friend Sarah, who was a number of yards down the aisle, sitting in the dust, eating her lunch-pail meal with another girl. "Sarah, do you have an extra hairpin? I can't seem to get mine back up the way I should!"

Mr. Lance, who was standing not far behind Sarah, finally looked in Abigail's direction. He crossed his arms and licked his lips. One eyebrow went up.

Sarah called back, "No, I don't have an extra. You best make do with what you have. The frames will be going again in just a minute."

Patrick grabbed Abigail's hand. "Listen to me, Abigail! Mr. Lance is a bad man!"

Abigail twisted away and said, "You don't know anything! Leave me alone! You aren't Father!"

"I know I'm not! But you're my sister!"

Mr. Lance stepped around Sarah, coming toward them. Lunch was nearly over. Operatives all along the aisle stood up, brushing themselves off, stretching arms overhead, readying themselves for the next long hours of work.

"Get out of here, Patrick," Liam said. "Go back to your own work. We are mad at you."

Mr. Lance's eyes winked. He was staring directly at Abigail. It was all Patrick could do to keep from lunging around his sister and driving his fist into the man's face.

Abigail pretended not to see Mr. Lance noticing her.

"Mr. Lance," Patrick said, standing, clenching his fists so he wouldn't lose his nerve, "I must talk with you. Right away."

Mr. Lance looked from Abigail to Patrick and his expression changed. "Hey, there," he said, lifting a finger and shaking it. "Are you supposed to be here today?"

Abigail glanced at Patrick, her face full of horror. "Patrick!"

"This will be brief, Mr. Lance. It's quite important. Please, step back with me for a moment."

Mr. Lance put his hands on his hips. "I beg your pardon, boy?"

Patrick crushed his hands into fists. "Don't beg my pardon. Just listen to me!"

Mr. Lance brushed by Abigail and stopped directly in front of Patrick.

"Boy." The condescension in the voice drew angry sweat from Patrick's arms, but he held his ground. "How can you still stand there when you've been spoken to? You best do what you're told. Get on now!"

"I'm not a mill rat," said Patrick. "In spite of what Mary Clatterbuck says."

The man almost laughed. "What are you talking about?"

"We aren't mill rats!" said Patrick.

"Go, Patrick!" said Liam. The little brother was

trying to be the big brother now. "Go downstairs where you belong!"

"Listen to your brother," said Mr. Lance.

Abigail's face twitched with anger, disappointment.

But Patrick trained his stare on Mr. Lance and in a low, controlled voice said, "Stay clear of my sister!"

Mr. Lance's jaw dropped open. "What did you say?"

"I said I know about the girl you got pregnant. Have there been others, or do you even care? You stay away from my sister." Patrick's blood rushed in his veins. His breathing came in shallow, sharp bursts.

The man roared then, like a lion, and he slapped Patrick with his open hand. "Insubordinate fool!" he shouted. Patrick stumbled, but held his ground. Suddenly the gears along the ceiling kicked into motion, and with deafening thunder the leather belts began to whirl, and the machines began to spin.

Mr. Lance grabbed Patrick by the arm, meaning to throw him down the aisle. But Patrick ducked and shoved, slamming his fists into the second hand's stomach. Mr. Lance stumbled over Liam and into Abigail.

"*No!*" Patrick screamed.

Abigail's long hair billowed as Mr. Lance bumped her and she tumbled backward. She fell against the corner of a spinning frame, and her hair was caught in the whirling leather belt. Her head snapped and an airy whistle issued from her mouth. A huge hank of hair ripped from her head and went up toward the ceiling, tangled in the still-moving belt.

And then Abigail fell, limp, to the floor.

"God, no!" Patrick ran to his sister and dropped on his knees. There were others around him instantly, Liam, Sarah, Rebecca, and operatives he didn't know. But he couldn't see them. He could only feel them. Could feel their disbelief and their horror. He laced his arm around his sister and lifted her to his chest. She was warm. She was still.

He raised his head to the ceiling, his eyes closing. "Oh my God, no!" And then his face fell and he buried it against Abigail's neck. He wanted to shake her, to shout at her, "Stay low! Watch out! Be careful and come home with us to our flat!"

But she didn't move.

Liam grabbed on to Abigail then, his shoulders convulsing. His hands clutched his sister as if to squeeze the life back into her.

Someone took Patrick's arms and lifted him up. He couldn't fight, he had no strength. There was screaming and crying around him now; he could hear it because the belts had been stopped and the machines silenced.

And then he heard Mr. Lance say, "Get her out of here. Careless idiots, her whole family! You all saw what happened. It wasn't my fault! Get her out of here! And that meddling brother, as well! We have an evening's work to do!"

Patrick felt himself release Abigail as Sarah and Rebecca and an old man, a machine mender, lifted her up to carry her out.

But then his mind shut down and he was running and he felt nothing, nothing at all. And even the demons screaming at his back couldn't keep up.

❧ 28 ❧

H<small>E STOOD ON</small> the Clatterbuck porch. He didn't remember getting there, but there he was, tears and sweat drying on his face, leaving salty tracks, his clothes filthy not only from mill dirt, but from times, he guessed, he'd fallen on his way. There was a hole in the right knee of his trousers, and a spot of blood within.

He pounded on the door.

An old woman in a cleaning apron answered. "May I help you?" But before Patrick could speak, Mrs. Clatterbuck was at the door, pushing the old woman aside. Her face, lit up with expectation, dropped when she saw Patrick.

"And what business do you have here in the middle of the day? You're Lucy's boy, aren't you?"

Patrick said, "I need to see my mother."

Mrs. Clatterbuck put one hand on her hip. A white-gloved hand touched her lips, then the bridge of her nose. She scowled. "Lucy's employed. She has her work. You'll have to wait until she is given her leave this evening."

Patrick's breathing quickened. He could see someone moving behind Mrs. Clatterbuck, peeking over her shoulder to see who was at the door. It was Nancy. Patrick said, "I need to see my mother. Now."

"Don't use that tone with me," said Mrs. Clatterbuck. "I'm the mistress here. I said you'll have to wait."

"Now."

"I'm closing the door, boy! Go away!"

"No! I want to see her now!"

Nancy brushed past her mother and stepped into the doorway. She said, "Patrick, isn't it?"

"Nancy!" said Mrs. Clatterbuck. "How dare you push me!"

"I didn't push, Mother, I merely mean to have conversation with Patrick. And, Molly," Nancy said to the old woman in the apron, "go get Mrs. O'Neill. She is in the backyard. Patrick needs to talk with her."

"Come inside and shut that door, Nancy!" Mrs. Clatterbuck demanded.

"Mother," said Nancy, "you've been worried all morning about the construction of your new pantry. Would you please go back to supervise?"

With a huff, Mrs. Clatterbuck gave Patrick one last look, then turned and disappeared down the shadowed hallway. Nancy came out to the porch, shaking her head. "Your mother will be here momentarily. I'm sorry about my own mother. She's in a tizzy. We had yet another robbery last night, but Father was much quicker this time. The thief was brought down

with a bullet to the thigh. The police have him in
custody."

James, oh, God, not you, too.

"Oh, don't worry, we're all fine," said Nancy. "No
one hurt, nothing taken this time. But the thief was
young. And to have ruined his life so soon. A shame,
really, although Mother would throttle me for
having pity on a burglar. We may be of the same
blood, but often I find we aren't of the same heart.
But you, Patrick?" She paused, as if she was seeing
Patrick's condition clearly at last. "You're hurt there,
on your knee."

Patrick knew he was bleeding, but he didn't feel
it. The only ache was in the palms of his hands, and
in his chest, his heart. He took a breath and said,
"Yes."

And then Lucy was at the door, standing half in,
half out, wiping her hands on the bottom of her
apron, her forehead lined with a scowl. Nancy with-
drew without another word.

"What is it, Patrick? You've left work? You haven't
quit there, have you?"

"No," said Patrick.

"No? Then why are you here? We've both work to
do!"

"Abigail's dead."

Lucy came out to the porch, her eyes never leaving Patrick's. The hem of her apron dropped. The
corners of her mouth flinched, but there was no
other sign she'd heard. She pulled the front door
closed behind her. "What are you saying, son?"

"Neck broke, caught in a belt. I was there. There
was a fight, and the second hand knocked her back.

I . . ." He swallowed. His throat was full of dry pebbles. "Mother, she's gone."

"Gone?"

"Yes." And Patrick stepped to his mother and folded into her, his arms wrapping her neck, his face against her shoulder. The sobs came, relentless, swollen and aching. He cried without relief, his soul twisting itself inside out, his body craving motherly caresses to help ease the agony.

But Lucy merely stood, and after a minute, she pushed Patrick away. Her eyes were closed, her mouth parted slightly. She shivered, as if shaking off a sudden chill, and then her eyes opened. But there were no tears.

"We can't change what's done," said Lucy. "I'll take a few days off and we'll see Abigail has a proper burial. But I will have no more crying. Longing does no good."

"We must go on, right, Mother?" said Patrick, hot, bitter sarcasm stinging his voice.

Lucy nodded, and touched her son's shoulder. This was the best she could do, Patrick knew. His heart was hollow. "I'll ask for leave," she said. "I'll be home soon. Wait for me there, and we'll make the arrangements. We will keep the apron Abigail wore when this happened, in her honor. It always bothered me that the army sent your father home in his civilian clothes."

What are you talking about? How on earth could this matter, Mother?

"My family always kept a piece of clothing that the deceased was wearing. It was our tradition. But the army kept his uniform. I didn't get it. Not his boots, nor his jacket. Not even a Union cap." She touched her lip, then went inside.

Patrick slowly walked down the porch steps to the walk. He could barely lift his head, it was so heavy.

Then a voice from the porch said, "I heard what you said, Patrick. I'm so very sorry! Is there anything I can do?"

Patrick looked back at Nancy. She was just outside the door.

"There's nothing anyone can do," said Patrick.

"Are you certain? Surely there must be—"

"No, there isn't," said Patrick. Then, because his mother would have expected politeness even now, he added, "But thank you just the same."

Nancy went back into the house without another word.

29

PATRICK STARED UP at the silver sliver of sky beyond the trees. There, occasional clouds drifted by, and the moon, a tiny white outsider in the daylight, held still and waited.

It waited for Patrick's decision.

And the decision came with a sigh, a drooping of the shoulders, and a painful core of resignation in Patrick's heart.

"I'll go away," he said to himself. He looked back down, across the lawn to the Clatterbucks' porch, speaking as though his mother were listening. "I'm going away, Mother. I'm going west. What is there here for me now? Abigail is dead. My best friend arrested, to be tried soon for robbery. Liam is angry at me, and you are strong enough to survive any loss. What would be another one?"

Patrick watched as sunlight winked through tree leaves, sparkling silver on the grass of the Clatterbucks' lawn. "If I'd kept the dragon lamp James had offered me, I could have sold it," he murmured. "It would have been enough to get on the train Polly Bruce has talked about so much and travel across the country."

The silver light winked at him as if it agreed.

"I should leave. It will be better for everyone. They will survive. If only I'd kept the lamp."

Then he thought of Mrs. Wilson's tea set. It was the answer. It was valuable.

"I'll miss Liam and Mother," he said. "I'll miss Mrs. Wilson and James. But I can't let that matter. I don't have any other choice."

There was one good thing he could do before he was gone. It wouldn't make up for the lies and the cowardice, but at least it was something. Moving away from the tree, Patrick sneaked around to the back of the Clatterbuck house, hiding in the shrubbery just outside their fence line. He skirted the corner, passed the compost pile, and walked quietly over the graveled pathway to the small, bare ground paddock. He knew he should be nervous, with the chance that Jed or John or even Mary would see him. But he couldn't feel anything except the need to do this, his one last good act before he sealed himself as a proven scoundrel.

Carefully opening the corral gate, Patrick stepped inside. Instantly the ponies stuck their heads out of their stalls and nickered. "Shh," he whispered.

At least there will be something Father could have been proud of, he thought. He crept to the first stall and unlatched it, then glanced down at the stall's floor. Jed had been right. The straw was old and beginning to mold. There was a dreadful smell, thick and foul.

The pony's legs were coated with manure.

"Run," Patrick said softly, waving his hand. "Run away and be free!"

The pony shivered, its eyes growing wide, then suddenly bolted from the stall, out into the corral, where it circled twice, then through the gate. It vanished between the trees that led to the river.

Quickly Patrick opened the other four stall doors. "Go," he ordered. "Run away while you have the chance!" Two others raced out, streaking through the gate, disappearing with tails held high.

Yes, Patrick thought as he watched them. *They're free. Someone will find them and care for them. But they're no longer at the mercy of people who have forgotten their conditions.*

He looked back. Two ponies, the chestnut and the dun, still stood in their stalls. They snorted and stomped, but were clearly too afraid to go outside. "Run," Patrick urged. "Here is your chance!" But they wouldn't go, even when he flapped his arms and clucked his tongue.

"Have you accepted this lot in life? Do you think there is no better?" he asked them.

The Clatterbucks' back door slammed shut. Patrick dropped to his knees and peered at the house through the fence slats. Emily was coming down the steps with a bucket of kitchen scraps. In a moment she'd be at the compost pile and would see him for certain.

Without looking back at the two ponies, he scuttled through the corral gate on hands and knees, over the gravel path, then stood and ran along the shrubs back to the front of the house and the tree-shaded lane.

As he straightened and glanced over his shoulder to assure himself that he hadn't been seen, he thought, *Father, this is all I can offer. You were a fighter, I am not. I'm sorry. I hope you won't know what I'm going to do now.*

Then he let his mind shut down, blocking out anything but the feel of his feet carrying him forward into town, up toward the tenements along Charlotte and the old woman's second-floor flat.

30

Mrs. Wilson wasn't home. It was a small miracle that he couldn't have hoped for. He knocked for a full minute, but received no answer. She was most likely at the market, or at the company store. Patrick could have gone in with Mrs. Wilson there, of course, and sneaked it beneath his shirt, but breaking into the flat would be easier because he wouldn't have to see her again.

Down on Charlotte Street, Patrick could hear the first of the operatives returning home from their long day at the mill. It was after seven o'clock. He would have to hurry. A swift kick against the doorknob and he knew the weak board would give way. On his head was the Union cap.

Then it would be a matter of a few seconds to go in, cram the silver tea set, a few doilies, some of the old teacups, and anything else he could grab beneath his shirt, and leave. Surely he'd get more than nineteen dollars for the whole of it from someone in a nearby town. And the train would be waiting; he would make his escape.

And what of the nineteen dollars in the wall of his own bedroom? Going back was out of the question. Mother and Liam were there. He did not want to see them. He would write Lucy soon and let her know where the money was hidden. She would find use for the money.

He lifted his foot to drive it against Mrs. Wilson's door.

There were voices and footfall at the bottom of the steps outside. Patrick plunged forward with all his strength. With a sudden, single crack, the latch shattered and the door crashed open.

He stepped into the doorway and stopped.

It was there still, as sure as the moon and the river and the bell in the tower. Mrs. Wilson's dignity, her honesty.

Patrick couldn't cross the threshold. His fingers caught themselves on the frame; his feet planted themselves beneath him.

He tried to push himself forward but couldn't move.

"It's too late!" Patrick cried to nobody. "Too late for me! I have to go in."

And then there were people in the hall with him. Men, women, children, pressing around him, talking with each other, coughing, shuffling. Someone caught him by the arm and he looked around. It was a girl a little younger than Liam; the girl he had screamed at one night not long ago.

"Mister," the girl said. Her face was streaked with

dirt and tiny pieces of lint. She must be a sweeper. "You visiting Mrs. Wilson?"

Patrick nodded. The cap felt very tight on his head.

The girl said, "Mrs. Wilson writes good, and I need her to do something for me. May I come in and talk with her?"

"She's not home."

"Then would you tell her something, please?" The girl paused, glanced down at her shoes, then looked back into Patrick's eyes. "Tell her would she write a letter to my mama for me? I want to go home and live with her. A girl was killed today, up in a spinning room. Broke her neck! They want to move me there to take her place." The girl shuddered. It was all she could do to finish her request. "They say I'm old enough to learn the frames. But I'm afraid! It won't change and I'll be killed, too! Please, tell Mrs. Wilson to write my mama. She's wrote her before. It's not too late if she will write it tonight. Will you ask her for me? I'm Anna Sewell."

"Yes."

"I wish I could write," the girl said solemnly. "There's so much can be done with words on paper."

"Yes."

The girl's eyes closed briefly as if in a thank-you. Then she said, "I'll come back after my chores and maybe she'll have the letter ready?"

"Maybe she will," said Patrick.

The girl followed the others down the hall. Patrick slowly pulled Mrs. Wilson's ruined door closed and went down to the street. He sat on the edge of a horse trough.

"A simple letter can save Anna Sewell's life," he said to himself. "Writing can be powerful indeed. I can write. I am stuck here in Leeland, where everything continues like it has been since the mill was built. But I can write."

He sat straight.

"*The Workers' Voice* said writers were needed. I could do that. I could share my thoughts with others besides myself and make a difference at the mill. Maybe I won't be making more money. Maybe I'll never get to college. But my writing can make a difference."

In the packing room he had heard a man say, "Strength in numbers!" This was true for a factory, true for a turnout. It was true for an army. It could be true for a band of renegade newspaper writers, as well.

Patrick dipped his hand into the trough and rubbed the water on his neck. It was cool and calming on his skin. He pulled the cap from his head and traced his finger on the inside band.

There was writing inside. It was pale and faded. Patrick squinted, holding it up and trying to see more clearly. The smudged ink looked as if it spelled "O'Neill."

Impossible.

Patrick's heart stood still. Was this his father's cap, taken from him before his body was sent home? Was this his father's way of letting him know he was still with him, still watching?

"Impossible," he said softly. "This is most likely

'some other man's hat, some other man whose name begins with an *O*. But it doesn't matter. As it might be another man's, it might also be my father's. I can believe what I want."

Patrick grinned and hugged the cap. His father, a soldier of the army, was still with Patrick, who would soon be a soldier of the word.

And then someone tapped his arm and he spun about. Mrs. Wilson stood there, a bonnet shading her face, a smile on her lips.

Patrick said, "A little girl named Anna wants you to write a letter to her mother about her going home. Will you find her and take her letter down for her?"

Mrs. Wilson nodded.

Then Patrick said, "Mrs. Wilson, I have to tell you something terrible. You will probably never want me to visit again, but I must be truthful with you."

Mrs. Wilson smiled and tipped her head in a question.

Patrick said, "You've been so kind to me. Too kind. I wanted to take advantage of your kindness. I tried to rob you."

Mrs. Wilson waved her hand in the air. It said, "Be quiet and follow me." Still smiling, she climbed the steps to her apartment. Patrick followed, scrambling to find the words to explain. He would show her the door, tell her what he'd done, and ask her forgiveness. It was another beginning.

Mrs. Wilson paused briefly at the shattered door, then went inside and sat in her chair. She picked up pen and paper and began writing. Patrick sat in his chair. He said, "Mrs. Wilson, please listen to me. Stop writing and listen."

Mrs. Wilson held up her hand for him to be quiet, then returned to her scribbling.

"No." said Patrick. "I must explain, although no explanation can be an excuse. I broke your door. I was going to rob you." He paused, watching her, hoping for something. Not absolution but acknowledgment, something. But she didn't look up. She kept on writing.

He said, "I hate the mill; you know that. I wanted to go to college. My sister . . ." He felt his voice quivering, but he fought his way through it. "My sister was killed today. I came to rob you and run off. Mrs. Wilson, I don't ask forgiveness. I just wanted to tell you."

There was silence, and it stretched uncomfortably long. Patrick linked his fingers around his knees and waited. "I'll fix your door," he said.

She worked on the note, head nodding in rhythm with the pen strokes.

Patrick sat and watched. Mrs. Wilson was likely writing a tirade, and one he deserved. He would take it as he would take foul medicine if the ailment required it.

She finally put her pen down and held out the note. Patrick took it, blinked, and read.

Patrick, hush about trying to rob me. You didn't do it. Only that door is ruined, but it's so dry-rotted I've needed another for a long time. This will give my son the incentive to find a new door. The tea set is gone as you can see, but you didn't take it.

Patrick looked up. The tea set was indeed gone. Where was it? Had someone else stolen it? He continued reading.

I sold the tea set and some other silver this morning. I need my medicine, and Andrew's pay can't always keep up. Medicine is more important than silver when you're growing old and feeble.

Patrick looked up at her, then back at the note.

But I wanted to give you something, too. Andrew never married. I'll never have grandchildren, as he is my only son. After the Pemberton incident, we both became so cautious about so much in life. I love him, but any thoughts he may have had about improving his life's condition became stagnant. But ever since I first saw you out on the street, I've come to think of you as a son. First because you look like Andrew, and then because you were considerate of me. Many young people don't give old people attention. You were nice to me.

Patrick's pulse picked up its pace. The corners of his eyes began to blur, but he read on.

I received $40 for the silver tea set and several other family items I took to the jeweler's. I want to give you half. It's not much, but maybe you can put it to good use. Maybe it will help get you to college someday. Take it, with my love.

Patrick couldn't look up. He was crying and didn't want her to see. He said, "Thank you, Mrs. Wilson."

He heard her write. Then she stood on her old knotted legs and came over to Patrick. She put the note in his lap.

I am so very sorry about your sister. Is there anything I can do?

After a moment, he lifted his face. It was tear-streaked, but suddenly he didn't care. He said, "You already have. And I'll make you proud of me."

Mrs. Wilson patted his hand.

"I really will."

31

He FOUND ROBBIE in the shed where James had left her. She gasped in shock and panic, but when he spoke, she slumped back on her wool blanket and turned away.

"Robbie, I'm so glad you're still here," Patrick said. "James told me where you were hiding, but I was afraid you would be gone when I got here. Or worse."

"Worse?" she said, her voice muffled in the darkness. The sun had set outside, and only pale street gaslight filtered through the small shed windows. "What, that I'd died? I'm too ornery for that."

Patrick eased the shed door shut, squinting, his eyes finally making sense of the shapes in the shed. He knelt down on the bare ground amid the tools and building implements. A cobweb crossed his face and he scratched it off. "I want to help you, Robbie. How is your arm?"

"Why do you want to help? You've got a family to

worry about, you have a job. I'm nothing to you."

"You're a friend."

Robbie rolled over and looked at him. "Friend? I don't have friends. James never came back and I think he's run off on me."

"No. He's arrested."

"Oh, God."

Patrick said, "Can you walk?"

"I don't know."

He put his arms under hers, glad she didn't fight him. He helped her, limping, to the door and out into the sunshine.

"Where are you taking me, Patrick? To the police to be with James?"

"To a doctor on Burris Street."

"I haven't any money! I can't trade the gimcracks in this shed or they'll know me as a thief, and James didn't have time to sell them properly." She was shaking fiercely.

Patrick said, "Don't worry. I have a little extra money. Just lean into me. I'll get you there safely."

Robbie hesitated, then put her head on Patrick's shoulder. "He will not be willing to see me. It's nighttime."

"We'll knock until he answers. We'll make him listen."

"And you'll pay for me?"

"Yes."

He felt her relax. And his heart soared.

32

September 23, 1870

The air is beginning to feel like autumn. I can smell something on the breeze, not the brisk, sharp scents of the country but a change, nonetheless. There is a crispness, an urgency, in this air. I welcome it.

My family is asleep at last, behind me in our flat. Mother was first to succumb; Liam followed not long after. It is nearing midnight. I'll try to sleep very soon.

Abigail rests in the public mortuary. We certainly cannot have a wake here; there is no room. Mother was agitated at having Abigail's body rest for a night where no one knows her, but tomorrow there will be a burial outside of town where the Irish and Canadians lay their own dead to rest. Tomorrow we'll bid her farewell and, as Mother says, go on. We are going to keep her apron as Mother requested; the rest we will give to the poor.

I'll miss her so.

Dear Abigail. She, too, had her dreams.

But for those of us who remain, there is work to do. There is a battle to fight. I will wage it with my written words. After this journal entry, there are two more things I must write before I go to bed. First, petitions to strike on behalf of Abigail. Liam and I will take them tomorrow and get them to as many as possible who can sign their names or mark their X. Then I will write an article for The Worker's Voice. *There are things to do now, things that feel good and strong and right.*

I wish James were here, to sit by me and chide me with his good humor. What will become of him, I don't know. I have never loved a friend as much.

But I believe Robbie will be all right. The doctor treated her arm wound with the incentive of a few dollars, even though he was in his nightshirt and cap and yawned several times during the treatment. When we were back on the street afterwards, I asked if she would come live with us. We've got an extra cot. But she said she didn't know, and vanished without another word.

My invitation remains open. I hope she will reconsider. If so, I hope Mother and Liam will accept her. I like to think they will.

Will anyone in the years that come read my journal, the letters I will write, the stories I plan to pen about our struggles here? Will they understand?

Patrick paused, looked up at the night sky, tilted his head, and nodded slowly.

The moon watches me still, as it has my whole life. But tonight it is not sneering. It is not taunting.
Tonight the moon is smiling.

Available by mail from

TOR
FORGE

1812 • David Nevin
The War of 1812 would either make America a global power sweeping to the pacific or break it into small pieces bound to mighty England. Only the courage of James Madison, Andrew Jackson, and their wives could determine the nation's fate.

PRIDE OF LIONS • Morgan Llywelyn
Pride of Lions, the sequel to the immensely popular *Lion of Ireland*, is a stunningly realistic novel of the dreams and bloodshed, passion and treachery, of eleventh-century Ireland and its lusty people.

WALTZING IN RAGTIME • Eileen Charbonneau
The daughter of a lumber baron is struggling to make it as a journalist in turn-of-the-century San Francisco when she meets ranger Matthew Hart, whose passion for nature challenges her deepest held beliefs.

BUFFALO SOLDIERS • Tom Willard
Former slaves had proven they could fight valiantly for their freedom, but In the West they were to fight for the freedom and security of the white settlers who often despised them.

THIN MOON AND COLD MIST • Kathleen O'Neal Gear
Robin Heatherton, a spy for the Confederacy, flees with her son to the Colorado Territory, hoping to escape from Union Army Major Corley, obsessed with her ever since her espionage work led to the death of his brother.

SEMINOLE SONG • Vella Munn
"As the U.S. Army surrounds their reservation in the Florida Everglades, a Seminole warrior chief clings to the slave girl who once saved his life after fleeing from her master, a wife-murderer who is out for blood." —*Hot Picks*

THE OVERLAND TRAIL • Wendi Lee
Based on the authentic diaries of the women who crossed the country in the late 1840s. America, a widowed pioneer, and Dancing Feather, a young Paiute, set out to recover America's kidnapped infant daughter—and to forge a bridge between their two worlds.

Available from Tor Classics

TOR®

THE LEGEND OF SLEEPY HOLLOW
Washington Irving
0-812-50475-5 • $2.99 ($3.99 CAN)

THE ADVENTURES OF TOM SAWYER
Mark Twain
0-812-50420-8 • $2.99 ($3.99 CAN)

WHITE FANG
Jack London
0-812-50512-3 • $2.99 ($3.99 CAN)

A CHRISTMAS CAROL
Charles Dickens
0-812-50434-8 • $2.99 ($3.99 CAN)

AGE OF INNOCENCE
Edith Wharton
0-812-56710-2 • $4.99 ($6.50 CAN)

PERSUASION
Jane Austen
0-812-56588-6 • $2.99 ($3.99 CAN)